Places didn't usually affect her this way.

Even the people she met were viewed as transient in her life, only a select few gaining the appellation "friend." Moving on had never been difficult and in fact was something she looked forward to, but she wasn't sure it was going to be that easy leaving here.

However, that wasn't something she had to think about for a while yet, especially since she didn't always plan her adventures in advance.

And, she reminded herself, for probably the two hundredth time over the last few weeks, just because Dr. Massimo Bianchi did funny things to her insides whenever she saw him was no reason to act on the attraction. In fact, considering all the other feelings she had about Minori and its surroundings, she was better off pushing that particular complication aside!

Yet it had been a long, fraught couple of months. Each time their eyes met, she had to fight off the memories of being in his arms. Of the way he'd touched her—both tenderly and roughly, the juxtaposition more arousing than anything she'd felt before—and the intensity of the pleasure he'd given.

Dear Reader,

Do you have a list of places you really want to visit? I do! One high on my list is the Amalfi Coast. From the first moment I saw a picture of that somehow-compelling rocky area, I've wanted to experience it for myself. Where better, then, to set this book, especially in light of my inability to travel right now?

And once that idea entered my mind, the hero made his abiding love for that glorious part of Italy known. Then the heroine interrupted, telling me that she too had wanted to visit Italy for absolute *ages*... Wouldn't I take her there?

Yes, my friends, sometimes my characters whisper to me, even before I've started writing, which is how I got to know quiet, intense Massimo and laughing, passionate Kendra. These two took me on a rather wild ride at a time of my life when I absolutely needed the sweet distraction of parsing out their hopes, fears and desires.

So I hope their journey together takes you away from reality, just for a while, and that you'll love them and *One-Night Fling in Positano* as much I loved bringing this book to life.

Ann McIntosh

ONE-NIGHT FLING IN POSITANO

———

ANN McINTOSH

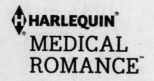

HARLEQUIN®
MEDICAL ROMANCE™

Recycling programs for this product may not exist in your area.

ISBN-13: 978-1-335-73728-1

One-Night Fling in Positano

Copyright © 2022 by Ann McIntosh

All rights reserved. No part of this book may be used or reproduced in any manner whatsoever without written permission except in the case of brief quotations embodied in critical articles and reviews.

This is a work of fiction. Names, characters, places and incidents are either the product of the author's imagination or are used fictitiously. Any resemblance to actual persons, living or dead, businesses, companies, events or locales is entirely coincidental.

For questions and comments about the quality of this book, please contact us at CustomerService@Harlequin.com.

Harlequin Enterprises ULC
22 Adelaide St. West, 41st Floor
Toronto, Ontario M5H 4E3, Canada
www.Harlequin.com

Printed in U.S.A.

Ann McIntosh was born in the tropics, lived in the frozen north for a number of years and now resides in sunny central Florida with her husband. She's a proud mama to three grown children, loves tea, crafting, animals (except reptiles!), bacon and the ocean. She believes in the power of romance to heal, inspire and provide hope in our complex world.

Books by Ann McIntosh

Harlequin Medical Romance

A Summer in São Paulo
Awakened by Her Brooding Brazilian

The Surgeon's One Night to Forever
Surgeon Prince, Cinderella Bride
The Nurse's Christmas Temptation
Best Friend to Doctor Right
Christmas with Her Lost-and-Found Lover
Night Shifts with the Miami Doc
Island Fling with the Surgeon
Christmas Miracle in Jamaica
How to Heal the Surgeon's Heart

Visit the Author Profile page at Harlequin.com.

For all who long to wander but have found their way impeded. And for Nic, whose unfailing belief in me means more than she can ever know!

CHAPTER ONE

THE PATH TO Spiaggia Tordigliano wasn't easy to find, but luckily Kendra Johnson had help in the form of Lejla and Ahmed Graovac, who knew the beach well.

"The top of the trail isn't on most maps," Ahmed explained, as they made their way down the narrow, stony path. "It's more of a local beach, popular especially with boaters, and not that many tourists come here, even in the high season."

That was exactly the type of place Kendra had asked the Graovac siblings to tell her about after meeting them in Naples and striking up conversation. In her experience, it was far better to go to the places the locals did. That was when you got the real flavor of an area or country.

What she hadn't expected was that the siblings would take the day off in the middle of the week to take her sightseeing.

"There isn't much to do right now," Lejla explained, when Kendra asked if she didn't have to be at work. "The owner of the café where I waitress will probably be happy not to have to pay me. Once the tourists start coming, though, I'll be working nonstop."

"And I want to practice my English," Ahmed interjected, sending Kendra a brilliant smile. "If I make it better, it will be easier to find work."

"How about you speak English, and I'll answer in Italian," she suggested, grinning back. "I need to practice for my upcoming job."

Which was how she ended up on the small path winding down from the main road toward the sea, tall grasses on either side brushing her legs and a fresh spring breeze blowing up from below.

"Tell me about Canada," Ahmed said, slowing down so that Kendra caught up to him.

"Don't mind him," Lejla interjected. "He's obsessed with North America. Keeps talking about going there to live."

"Not North America. Canada," her brother replied, sending her a scowl. "I heard that Canada is a polite, beautiful place, and one day I want to see it for myself. All of it. Polar bears. Everything."

Kendra chuckled. "That would take you a very long time. Canada is a huge country."

"Maybe so. But I hear from my friend's cousin who lives there that it is wonderful. Full of opportunity."

Not wanting to burst his bubble but trying to

be honest, Kendra replied, "It's not that different from other places I've been. There are all kinds of people everywhere, and opportunities for some, but not always for others."

In a way, she could understand Ahmed's enthusiasm for somewhere he'd never seen. Wasn't that the same impulse that kept her traveling from place to place, and made her a bit indifferent to her homeland?

Much of the last six years had been spent traveling to different countries, working a few months here, a few there, immersing herself in the various cultures. The worldwide pandemic had put her plan of working her way around as much of the world as possible on pause.

She'd been in Dubai when the worst of the virus hit, and luckily enough her contract teaching English had been extended, becoming a remote job. However, even with her students to talk to during the week, weathering the isolation had been difficult. Oh, she liked her alone time as much as the next person—probably more—but it had been the one time she'd wished she'd been back in Toronto. There, at least, she could possibly have formed a bubble with her aunt and cousins, or gone back to hospital work, doing her part to fight the virus.

Dubai was supposed to be just a short stop in a place she'd heard so much about but never visited. Planning to stay only a month or so, she hadn't applied for a work visa, or for a nursing job. Being offered the teaching position had been happenstance but she'd seen the four-month stint as a way to save up a bit more cash, and taken it. Instead, it had turned into almost total solitary confinement, lasting more than eighteen months.

How glad she was to be on the move again!

The job in the village of Minori, on the Italian Amalfi Coast, had come through at just the right moment. She'd gotten to Italy at the beginning of May, and her stint at the clinic was scheduled from the beginning of June to the end of October. Spending six months exploring this lovely country felt like heaven, and looking around at the bright springtime sky, Kendra couldn't help grinning.

Maybe it was the enforced confinement she'd just escaped that made her think it was the most beautiful day she'd ever seen.

"Italy isn't to my liking," Ahmed said, his nose wrinkling slightly. "Our parents should have tried to get to Canada when they fled Bosnia."

"They didn't have that option, Ahmed." If Lejla's tone was any indication, this wasn't the first time she'd heard her younger brother say so. "Don't be a brat."

Ahmed huffed, and sent his sister a glare. "We'd be better off if they had. And if I lived in

Canada I would never want to leave, the way I want to escape Italy."

Just then they turned a corner in the path and the vista below opened up.

Kendra stopped, her breath catching in her throat for a moment as a wave of emotion overtook her, causing the sound of the argument going on behind her to fade into insignificance.

The land and seascapes were a study in greens, grays and blues, bordered by the darkness of the rocks and sand, elevated to almost mythical splendor by the glint of sun on the water. Outside of the cove, on the open water, a fishing boat went by at what seemed a leisurely pace, the bright red of her hull adding the perfect splash of contrasting color. A little closer to shore a small sailboat tacked, the white of its sail like a friendly flag, waving.

There was no real comparison between the scene below and the coast of Nova Scotia, where she'd lived until she was ten, but a wash of longing made her eyes prickle anyway.

Open water, especially the sea, always spoke to her, no matter where she was. It was the voice of her childhood. Whatever mood it was in, whether murmuring, splashing or roaring, it took her back to a time of peace, contentment and joy. More than anything else, it made her think of Dad. Of his laughter, booming voice and sudden rages that never scared her because they were so transient—gone in a blink—with the laughter coming back right on their heels.

She'd gotten that from him. Both the temper and the tendency to laugh often, and she was glad of it. He'd been wonderful, and she missed him every day.

Losing him so young, she knew her memories were probably skewed, but no less precious for that fact. And the sea was equally precious, since it invariably brought those reminiscences back.

"And if I lived here," she whispered to herself, thinking about what Ahmed had said moments before, "I might never want to leave."

Still arguing in what she assumed was their native language, the Graovacs passed her and went down the path toward the beach, but Kendra wasn't ready to follow yet. Held in place by the stark, almost harsh beauty spread out before her, she took a deep breath of salty air and simply allowed herself to *feel*.

The cool, briny breeze against her face, overlaying the warmth of the sun.

An almost spiritual call of rocks that looked as though carved with a serrated blade, set against the dazzling blues of the water and sky.

With the stony grays and black sand, it should have been a dour scene, but it wasn't. Instead, for

Kendra, it evoked a strange, joyous recognition, although she'd never been here before.

The slap of the waves breaking, the rustle of the wind through the grass and the trill of a bird were the only sounds, now that her companions had moved out of earshot. A complete contrast to the fervent rush and noise of Naples, with its constant motion and chatter. While the city had provided all the friendly faces and excitement she'd been missing, the peace and tranquility here spoke directly to her soul.

"Mi scusi."

The deep voice, coming from directly behind her, startled Kendra out of her trance.

"Oh," she said, turning. But the apology she planned to proffer died on her tongue, as she looked up into a pair of midnight-dark eyes, and was once more washed with a nameless, unrecognizable emotion.

He wasn't really handsome. His face was too broad, his nose too beaky and his lips a tad too thin for him to be considered classically good-looking. His hair was as dark as his eyes, curling wildly in the ocean breeze, giving him a tousled, just-out-of-bed look. He was also tall and broad—barrel-chested and thick of trunk—but not, she thought, fat. Just a large, solid type of man, his shape very different from the body types worshipped in the fashion magazines or on the silver screen. The kind of man who would make even a woman as big-boned and hefty as herself feel feminine and, if not tiny, then perhaps *dainty*.

Effortlessly elegant, even in casual clothes, just one glance at him set Kendra's heart racing in the silliest way, and left her completely, utterly tongue-tied.

So, instead of trying to say another word, she stepped aside to let him pass.

With a murmured *"Grazie,"* he strode off down the path without a backward glance, while she stood there watching him until he disappeared.

Wondering when, if ever, her heart would return to a normal pace, and this sensation of light-headedness would go away.

"Kendra. Aren't you coming? We still need to get over to the other side where the beach is nicer."

"I'm coming," she called back to Ahmed, forcing her legs to move, when they really didn't feel strong enough to hold her up.

It was just the surprise of having that huge man sneak up on her, she told herself, as she followed her friend toward the rocks on the right-hand side of the beach.

Nothing more.

Although, she had to admit she'd been drawn to him in the weirdest way. That in itself was amusing, since on the whole the Italian men she'd met so far really hadn't piqued her interest. Not that there weren't some who were attractive. Even some whom she could honestly say were almost stunningly handsome. Yet, although she'd so far enjoyed the man-watching, not one pair of slumberous eyes or a wide, bright smile had given her pause.

Until now.

Mind you, with the way she was feeling, she wouldn't mind indulging herself with a night or two of passion. The last time she'd had sex...

She actually had to stop and think about it, to figure out how long it had actually been.

Maybe Mick, in Hong Kong?

He'd been a good, if uninspired, lover, who'd wanted her to stay there even though she'd been up-front with him about her plans to move on. It had certainly soured her last couple of weeks in the special administrative region of China, and she and Mick had parted on rather frosty terms.

At least on his side.

She didn't have the time or the energy to get upset with people, especially since she knew she wouldn't be around long enough for it to make a big difference in her life. However, she also wasn't in the habit of jollying people out of their snits.

That was all on them, and above her pay grade.

Climbing a ladder, and then scrambling over

the rocks, revealed the other side of Spiaggia Tordigliano. And there, already about halfway down the beach, was the man from the path, sitting on the sand, an open book on his lap.

Maybe if she wasn't with Ahmed and Lejla she'd have been tempted to mosey on down that way and interrupt his reading. Just the thought made her smile to herself. Daydreams and lust from a distance were all well and good, but she was wise enough, and careful enough, not to give in to that kind of impulse.

After all, he could be a wandering serial killer, for all she knew!

"What are you smiling about?" Ahmed sent her a curious look, as he held out a hand to help her down from the last rocky ledge.

Ignoring his silent offer of help, Kendra hopped down on her own, grinning back at him.

"Nothing really. It's just so beautiful here, I can't help smiling."

He cast his gaze around, and then shrugged slightly.

"It's okay, and I like that it's rarely full of people, but I'm sure you've seen more beautiful places."

Lejla had brought a blanket for them to sit on, and they spread it on the sand. Kendra kicked off her shoes and sat, then lay back, reclining up on her elbows so she could take in the ocean view and watch the sea ebb and flow onto the shore.

Three small motorboats were anchored in the bay, and the music and laughter of their inhabitants carried across the water. Ahmed was once more asking about Canada, and Kendra answered his questions while watching the waves. The sailboat she'd noticed earlier came back into view, closer to shore now, and she could see what looked like a man and a child in the vessel. Farther out at sea, a large luxury yacht was just disappearing around the headland.

The sailboat tacked again and then, as Kendra watched, the child moved from the bow and scrambled to where the man sat in the stern, and they began to switch places.

Probably a sailing lesson, she thought, smiling as she remembered going out with her own father for just the same purpose, and performing the same maneuver.

The child was in position, the man just turning to sit in the bow, when the boat rocked violently and the boom swung. Instinctively, she shouted a warning, watching in horror as the man was struck on the side of the head, and went over into the water.

Kendra was already on her feet, dark glasses tossed aside as she pulled her shirt off over her head.

"Kendra, what…?"

"Try to get someone to help the child in the boat," she said, making it an order, rather than a request. Lejla jumped to her feet and gave a strangled cry, obviously realizing what was happening, and pointed to where the sailboat headed out to sea, the child in it screaming for his or her father.

Kendra had her shorts off already and ran for the water, adrenaline pumping so her heart hammered and her focus narrowed to the last point where she'd seen the man.

The frigid water hardly registered as she ran in and then did a shallow dive. Her strong arms and legs, along with her training in water rescue, served her well in getting her out to where she thought she needed to be, but there was no sign of the boater.

Taking a deep breath, she dived, searching beneath the waves, turning in a circle, aware of the current wanting to pull her farther down, and away.

Nothing.

Stroking strongly to the surface, she took another breath, and dived again, now letting the current guide her, hoping it would drag her in the right direction.

There.

A shadow, sinking, floating away.

No time for another breath.

Swimming down, down, grabbing hold of an arm, then making for the sunlight that suddenly looked to be miles away.

When she finally broke the surface again, Kendra gasped in needed air, even while tugging the man's head above water, and arranging him in a rescue hold.

Then she was flutter-kicking, as hard as she could, back toward the shore, ignoring the almost sickening pounding of her heart, the ache in her lungs, her full concentration on keeping the man's face above water and getting him to dry land.

Something brushed against her arm, but before she could even think to be scared, a dark head hove into her line of sight. Surprised, Kendra's gaze collided with a pair of black, fathomless eyes set in a strong, square, instantly recognizable face.

There was no time to register much more than that, before that deep voice said, "Let me take him."

It took her a moment to interpret his words. Her Italian was passable, but she'd never considered having to use it under quite these circumstances, with her nerves jangling and her heart pounding so she could barely hear him.

"No."

She made her voice firm, adding a quick shake of her head for emphasis, and was pleased when he took her at her word. Rather than insist, he simply kept pace with her until she got to the shallows. Only then did he move to assist her to carry the man up onto the shore and place him on the ground, out of the way of the surf. Now Kendra could see the bruise to the boater's temple, and registered the fact that he didn't seem to be breathing.

She reached for the unconscious man's neck to feel for a pulse, but the man who'd swum out to assist her got to it first. Their hands brushed, and Kendra drew hers back quickly.

"I'm a doctor," the man said brusquely, not looking up from where he was focused, his long, thick fingers pressed against the other man's carotid. Bending, he put his ear close to the boater's face for a long moment.

"The ambulance is on the way," Lejla said, from behind Kendra's shoulder, her voice choked and scared. "And one of the motorboats is helping the child in the sailboat."

The doctor didn't answer, but positioned himself to begin chest compressions.

"I know CPR," Kendra said, realizing he had the situation well in hand, so there was really no need to tell him her own credentials as an RN. "I can help."

His gaze flashed up to her for an instant, and Kendra shivered.

"Grazie."

But there was little to do but watch as he set to work, performing the chest compressions with calm competence, counting as he did. Periodically he paused, and once more put his ear to the other man's face. Then he was back to it.

Kendra could hear the wail of sirens in the distance, just as the patient began to cough violently, and his child ran across the sand, shrieking, "Papa! Papa!"

It was a relief to be able to take hold of the little girl—as it turned out to be—and tell her, "Your papa is going to be all right. What is your name?"

"Isabella," she gasped out through her sobs.

It took a while for the ambulance attendants to get to the beach, but sooner than she'd expected, considering the route they had to take, they were running across the sand toward them.

The doctor looked up at Kendra to say, "I will accompany him in the ambulance." Turning his attention to Isabella, he said, "You will come with us too. We will take your *papa* to the hospital, and make him all better."

The gentleness of his tone when speaking to the child made a shiver run along Kendra's spine. Getting up to make way for the ambulance attendants, still holding Isabella close to her side, Kendra watched as the doctor also rose. He was giving the attendants their patient's information, but Kendra didn't hear any of it.

All she could do was stare at him, and the pounding of her heart now had nothing to do with her prior exertions.

He was a magnificent sight, his heavily muscled body moving with surprising fluidity as he jogged over to a pile of clothing dropped haphazardly on the sand. All he was wearing was a pair of boxer briefs, which, being wet, were molded to every plane and bulge of his lower torso and upper thighs.

Every.

Single.

Bulge.

All of which were impressive.

When he started shrugging into the blue, long-sleeved shirt, Kendra shivered again.

Why didn't I go and speak to him when I had the chance?

But having the crying little girl clinging to her side made most of the regret fade away. If she'd been concentrating on flirting, she probably wouldn't have seen the accident occur, and maybe the man now on the stretcher wouldn't have been saved.

Tearing her gaze away from where the doctor was struggling to put his pants on over his wet skin, she gave Isabella a tighter squeeze. Running her hand over the little girl's head, she made soothing noises, not trusting her befuddled brain to find the right words in Italian. Her insides were quaking like jelly, the combination of coming down from the adrenaline and her strange, visceral reaction to the man now striding toward her across the sand.

Their gazes met again, and those seemingly bottomless eyes made the vibrations in her belly intensify, until she knew if she didn't look away once more, her legs might just give out.

Taking a shaky breath, she turned to watch as the paramedics began to carry the stretcher over the sand.

"Come, little one." The deep rumble of his voice shot through Kendra's veins, disturbing her equilibrium even more. When he held out his hand to the little girl, Kendra clenched the fingers of her free hand, so as not to reach for it herself. "As for you," he said to Kendra, with not a hint of the tenderness he'd had for Isabella. "You need to get dry. You're shivering, and we already have one patient. We don't need another."

Kendra nodded, not willing to trust her voice, lest she tell him that just looking at him made her hot all over, and she didn't need a towel.

Then, at a shout from the ambulance attendants, now almost to the rocks, the connection between them was shattered, and Kendra took in a deep breath. The doctor picked up Isabella, and with one last nod started at a trot across the sand after them, and in moments was gone from sight.

But the memory of him lingered long after, leaving Kendra with a strange sense of life having changed, and a host of questions that started with, *What if...?*

CHAPTER TWO

Dr. Massimo Bianchi had a theory that Fate had a diabolical sense of humor. One that he didn't appreciate.

It really liked dangling things in front of him, only to yank them away again.

Which is why, as he looked across the café in Positano at the woman in the midst of a raucous group of people, he made no effort to go over and speak to her.

The last thing he needed was to stand there, tongue-tied, while everyone else around him chatted and laughed.

Only too well did he know what it felt like to be the odd man out—the one everyone else ignored. After all, he'd just left his parents' home, where all his ebullient relatives had laughed and chatted and shouted, not even trying to include him. That he was used to. He'd lived it most of his life. Being the middle child of seven and the only introvert in a large, extroverted family—the one teased for being studious instead of rambunctious—he knew when to keep to himself.

So, instead of exposing himself by going over to where the woman stood, he turned his attention back to the view spread out before him. Trying to achieve the peace sunset on the Amalfi Coast usually brought to his heart.

In his estimation, there could be nowhere as beautiful as the rugged coast, with the mountains and terraced farms above, and its tenacious villages clinging to the slopes. With both land and sea bathed as it was now in the golden glow of the sun sinking toward the horizon, it was the epitome of everything lovely.

Massimo found himself glancing back at the woman on the other side of the bar, and quickly pulled his gaze away again.

It was the second time he'd seen her in as many days, and he couldn't understand his reactions. Just looking at her made his muscles go rigid, his heart race and tumble.

He'd been testy for the last two days, ever since that first sight of her, at Spiaggia Tordigliano.

All he'd wanted was a quiet day away from the tension he always felt when visiting his family in Napoli. That sensation of being out of step with everyone. But instead of a relaxing beach visit, what he'd gotten was a jolt, akin to a punch straight to the solar plexus, which left him winded and confused. So much so that rather than stay at his parents' home until after the weekend, as originally planned, he'd felt the intense need to get away by himself for the rest of his vacation.

Suddenly the constant noise and hoopla in the house, the cacophony of cars and people in the city, had been too much to bear.

He was honest enough with himself to know the change from routine trip to the beach to emotional whirlwind had happened long before the drowning incident. In actual fact, it had started on the trail down to Spiaggia Tordigliano, when he'd come up behind that woman standing on the path.

Something about her straight-backed posture, the air of almost palpable joy in her stance, had kept him rooted where he stood. He'd almost expected her to throw open her arms, as though to embrace the scene before her, although she didn't move at all.

Her immobility had given him the opportunity to take in as much of her as he could see.

She was fairly tall and solidly built, with a beautifully shaped skull, broad shoulders and a torso that tapered in before flaring into wide hips. Smooth skin, chestnut-hued in the sun, reminded him of the finest silk. Her hair, an unusual shade of mingled walnut and honey, hung in a thick plait along her spine, and his fingers itched to touch it, and discover its texture. Long, strong legs and arms completed the picture, and although Massimo had always in the past been attracted to petite, willowy women, he'd found himself fascinated.

He'd very much wanted to see her face.

Making her aware of him elicited a sound of surprise, and she'd turned to look at him...

Cavolo!

Just the memory of seeing her face for the first time had Massimo muttering the oath under his breath, although at the time he'd bitten it back.

Her face was broad, with high, sharp cheekbones, and eyes of medium brown with an unusual shape—not quite oval but with a little droop at the corners that made them unbearably sexy. Those eyes had widened as she looked at him, and in them gleamed what appeared to be the same surprised recognition washing through his veins.

Yet he knew, without doubt, they'd never met before.

Then his gaze had fallen to her lips, which were lush—delicious—and slightly parted, as though she were about to speak, although she did not.

His entire body went hot, and tightened in a rush of need so intense he felt ever so slightly dizzy, and the shock of it had him hurrying past, when everything inside him shouted for him to stay. To ask her name.

To kiss that luscious mouth, even if to do so would land him in all kinds of crazy trouble.

He was not a man given to impulsiveness, so just having those thoughts even cross his mind propelled him to walk faster, so as to get away from the temptation she presented.

Yet, his mind had remained there, with her, and when the young man she was with called to her, Massimo's brain insisted on taking note of her name.

Kendra.

It suited her, but then his brain had so many questions that circled and whirred in his head.

Did she live in Italy, or was she a tourist?

If she were a tourist—and it was difficult to tell, since she'd answered her friend in fluent, if accented, Italian—where was she from?

And, as for the young man with her, was he her boyfriend, even though it was none of Massimo's business whether they were a couple or not?

All of those conflicting feelings had made his quiet day implode on itself, and although he'd pretended to be reading, his gaze had kept straying up the beach.

To her.

Which is how he was instantly aware when she shouted and jumped to her feet. As she stripped off her shirt and shorts, his brain could make no sense of any of it, until he heard the screams coming from the sailboat, and realized what must have happened.

By then Kendra was already running toward the water, dressed only in a sports bra and barely there panties.

Now that was an image seared into his mind for all times. One that he'd had to push aside while he tore off his own clothes and went into the sea after her.

He may as well not have bothered, since she was already on her way back to shore with the boater by the time he was halfway to the scene. Her cool, calm demeanor was truly impressive, as was her sheer physical strength.

It wasn't something he thought he'd ever find alluring, but there was no mistaking his feelings for anything but attraction.

Of course, all of that had to be put aside so as to help his patient, and there had been no time to do anything other than dress and, taking the patient's daughter, go after the paramedics. But it was impossible to forget the sight of her body, in no way concealed by her wet underwear.

Lovely full breasts and pebbled, dark nipples clearly visible through her bra.

Rounded, smooth belly, with the indentation of her navel begging to be laved by his tongue.

Those long, strong legs ending in tight, high buttocks that he wanted to palm. To squeeze.

The enticing mound, where a line of dark hair showed beneath her cotton panties.

Once more he'd wanted to kiss her, touch her, take her away to the nearest bed and discover what it would take to satiate her, over and over again.

While Massimo was glad the man rescued from the sea, Fortuno Demarco, was alive and doing well in the hospital, there was a part of him that had regretted the missed opportunity.

And now, there she was again.

But still he resisted the temptation.

His was not the type of demeanor suited to flirtation, and although there was no escaping her allure, he also was quite sure this was another of Fate's annoying little tricks.

Nothing good could come from speaking to her.

Then, as he was taking a sip of his *aperitivo*, there was a light touch on his shoulder, and a warm, slightly husky voice said, "*Dottore*, how is your patient?"

And he realized Fate was trying to bamboozle him once more.

How often did life give you a second chance?

Not nearly often enough in Kendra's book.

So, when it did, she was always the first one to jump all over it.

Risk-taking didn't bother her in the slightest. In fact, she often thought it was encoded in her DNA.

Yet, when the seated man put down his glass and turned those midnight eyes on her, something inside shivered out a warning.

"He should have been discharged from the hospital in Napoli today."

At the sound of his deep, quiet voice her mouth went dry, and her knees felt shaky. She licked her lips and, pulling out the other chair at the table, sat down. But she kept the smile firmly on her face, not wanting to reveal the strangely magnetic pull the doctor was exerting on her senses.

"So, no complications?"

That earned her a slight headshake, but his gaze never left her face. "None. In fact, after he was reassured of his daughter's safety, he immediately asked about his boat."

Amusement rippled through her, bringing a gust of laughter.

"Boys and their toys," she said in English, not able to translate it in her head into Italian.

The doctor smiled slightly, and the twinkle she saw in his eyes made a shiver of awareness trickle down her spine.

"Sì." He nodded. "Boys and their toys."

The sound of that alluring voice speaking English with a delicious Italian accent turned the shiver into a tremor of need deep in her belly.

"Are you a tourist?" he asked. "Or do you live in Italy?"

She knew better than to divulge information about herself to strangers, so, smile still firmly in place, she replied, "Oh, I'm just traveling through."

It wasn't a lie, really. She was traveling through Positano on her way to her new job, but he didn't have to know that detail.

"What other parts of Italy have you seen?"

He'd reverted to Italian, and Kendra did too.

"I've been to Rome, Venice and Florence, but didn't get to spend as much time as I'd have liked to. One day I'd like to go back and see more of them."

His gaze dropped for a moment, and Kendra realized he had the most amazingly long, thick eyelashes, which she'd somehow not noticed before, caught as she was by his dark, mysterious gaze. Why seeing those lashes made her breath hitch for a second, she wasn't quite sure.

"You liked Roma?"

There was something in his tone, a curious inflection she couldn't understand and found herself wanting to, but she answered honestly anyway.

"It certainly was vibrant and beautiful. And when you come from a country where people consider a three-hundred-year-old building a landmark, seeing the really ancient buildings and artifacts was stunning."

The corners of his mouth lifted, and Kendra lost her ability to breathe when she saw him smile fully for the first time.

He went from passably good-looking to sinfully handsome with that simple act, which caused deep slashes, like elongated dimples, in his cheeks. And she knew, right then, that she absolutely, positively wanted to have sex with this man.

How to initiate that, though, was the question.

"I can see how that may be true," he said, twisting his glass back and forth between his fingers, his gaze once more fixed on her face. "We tend to take such things for granted here."

Pulling herself together, keeping a slightly amused expression on her face, she nodded. "Seeing ancient sites reminds me of how fleeting life can be, and prompts me to keep enjoying the brief time we all have."

His eyebrows rose slightly. "You've seen many such places?"

Now this was a safe enough subject, and she leaned back into the chair, relaxing.

"Not all as ancient as the Colosseum, but I've

been to Angkor Wat and Lalibela, as well as a host of other places, like the Valley of the Kings and the Pyramids."

He tilted his head, the intensity of his gaze deepening. "You have traveled extensively."

"Yes. First for my job, and then because I wanted to."

"How many places have you visited?"

She could hear the curiosity in his tone, and it amused her. No one believed her when she told them the actual number, so she said, "Too many to count. Several African and Asian countries, Australia and New Zealand, and now I'm working my way through as much of Europe as I can manage."

"La voglia di girovagare."

It took her a moment to parse that out in her head, and then she laughed. "Yes, you're right. I do have wanderlust. Or perhaps more the desire to simply be a vagabond, never settling anywhere."

"What are you looking for, when you travel?"

The question took her aback. His tone gave it a meaning beyond the obvious, and opened up a space inside her she didn't want to explore. A sore spot on her soul.

Now it was hard to keep smiling, but she somehow achieved it.

"Adventure. Freedom. A wider worldview than

the one I grew up with, I think. It's in my blood, somehow, and I don't see any good reason to resist it."

"Fair enough." He tipped the rest of his drink into his mouth, giving her a lovely view of his strong neck, the motion of his Adam's apple giving her an awful thirst she couldn't deny. Putting down his glass, and as though hearing and misunderstanding her thought, he asked, "May I offer you a drink?"

She hesitated, turning the situation over in her mind, figuring it out to her satisfaction.

If the chance arose, she would make the first move to become intimate with him, and have no issue with doing so. But that wouldn't happen here, surrounded by other people, overlooked by the crowd.

Getting him alone might prove to be difficult, but she'd give it her best shot.

"Actually, I was going to go down on the beach to watch the sunset. Would you care to join me?"

It was his turn to hesitate, those bottomless eyes giving nothing away, but searching her face, as though trying to figure out her true intention for asking.

Then he nodded, just once, and pushed his chair back from the table.

"It would be my pleasure to accompany you,

on the condition that you allow me to buy you dinner after."

Kendra gave him her best and widest smile, and, as he eased her chair out from behind her and she stood, she suspected he was contemplating the same outcome to the evening she was.

"I'd love to."

CHAPTER THREE

MASSIMO SMILED AT the squirming, fussing toddler and hummed a little tune to distract him. The tactic worked, as it often did, and little Tommaso calmed a bit, his bright gaze affixed to Massimo's face. When Massimo began to sing a ditty popular with the two and under set, Tommaso actually laughed, and totally missed the fact he'd been inoculated.

"You're so good with the little ones," Mrs. Tarantella said, while Massimo was filling out Tommaso's vaccination form and she fought for supremacy over her son, who was once more wriggling, wanting to be put down. "When are you going to start a family of your own?"

It wasn't the first time he'd been asked such a question and, as he always did, Massimo just smiled, and replied, "Have you been speaking to my mother? She too is always asking."

He couldn't help hearing the little cough of laughter Fatima, the nurse assisting him, gave. Nor was it possible to avoid seeing the speculative gleam in Constancia Tarantella's eyes, as though she were mentally listing all her available female relatives. But, before she could continue that line of questioning, Massimo turned the conversation to Tommaso's next wellness visit, set for two months hence.

Mrs. Tarantella frowned.

"August is the busiest time of year for us," she said, shaking her head. "I might not be able to bring him then."

"Make time, please." Massimo made his voice firm, but softened the demand with a smile. "While Tommaso is doing well, because he was premature and had complications with his lungs it's important that we monitor him even more carefully than usual. He's still on the lower end of the height and weight percentiles, and there are milestones I want to make sure he is hitting as he grows."

With a marked reluctance, Mrs. Tarantella agreed to make the appointment, and soon after departed, her son straddling her hip and waving gleefully at Massimo and Fatima.

As he made the last of his notes, Fatima cleaned and sanitized the room in preparation for their next patient, humming the same tune Massimo had sung for Tommaso.

"Porca vacca," the nurse said, her tone some-

where between annoyed and amused. "Now that tune will be stuck in my head all day."

Massimo didn't comment, and Fatima probably didn't expect him to. Everyone at the clinic was used to his quiet ways.

"You must be tired of everyone trying to marry you off," the nurse said, as she sprayed down the examination table and began wiping it down. "Every woman who comes in here seems determined to find you a match. I'm sure Mrs. Tarantella asked you the same thing last time she brought Tommaso in."

What could he say to that? Even if he were inclined to comment, to say what he really felt about it would be far too revealing.

He no longer believed in the type of love he once dreamed of. The kind that was inescapable, all-encompassing and struck like lightning, sweeping all away in its path. Love that lasted eternal, and was reciprocated. Once upon a time he'd felt that thunderstruck sensation, and believed he'd found his one.

Therese had cured him of that notion, with one vicious indictment of everything he held dear.

"You're a stuffy old man already, Massimo, and not yet even thirty-five! How could I bear to spend my life with you, moldering away in this hole of a village?"

She hadn't cared that he loved Minori and the

Amalfi Coast. Or that he felt he was doing the work he was meant to. He didn't need—or even like—the bright city lights, preferring a quieter existence. Nor did he feel working in a small clinic was less important than working in a large hospital, or doing major surgeries.

In fact, the job he did was, in his view, equally important, since it served people sometimes an hour away from a hospital, or elderly folk who had difficulty getting around. If clinics like the one here in Minori didn't exist, what would those people do? And when they all flocked to Napoli or one of the other cities for treatment, those places would be overburdened.

But, for all that, he might have given in and gone with her, if it weren't for Nonna, whom he'd promised to help convert her small farm into an *agriturismo*. He'd given his word that he'd supervise the building of three villas on the property, and assist her to get the venture up and running, and his word was his bond, always.

Again, Therese hadn't cared.

"You're allowing that old witch to use you. You have six brothers and sisters. Why can't one of them come and help?"

If anyone ever asked him if he could describe love dying a horrible death, he'd reach back for the memory of that moment, and hearing those words. And, even if unable to articulate it, would still feel that sick, bottom-dropping-out-of-his-world sensation.

Could still feel it even now.

He could forgive her for all the things she'd said about him. He'd heard variations of that theme even from his own father most of his life. That he was boring, too cautious, too rigid and—on one memorable occasion—insipid when compared with his more colorful brothers and cousins. But what was unforgivable was Therese's attack on an elderly woman who'd done nothing but try to be good to her grandson's fiancée. In that moment, she'd shown the true ugliness that lay beneath her stunning exterior.

"It was just infatuation," Nonna had said, with a definitive nod. He'd never told her why the relationship had ended, too hurt and angry, and not wanting to cause her any pain. "One day you will discover the difference."

But his meeting and courting of Therese had been born of love, he was sure. Growing up on the stories of his parents' first encounter, Massimo had expected that rush of attraction, the falling sensation on first sight. Therese's sultry beauty, her come-hither eyes and sensual persona, had felled him in an instant, and he'd had the surety that this was the person meant to be his, forever. Having experienced *amore a prima vista*, and seeing it go so terribly wrong, he no longer believed love at first sight was the answer. Or perhaps even true.

For an instant, memories from just days ago rushed into his head...

"Ah..."

The gasp was followed by husky laughter, and a circling motion of the hips that made Massimo have to call on every ounce of control he had, so as not to explode inside her. Then she tightened her long, strong legs around him, as though to immobilize him.

"Wait. Wait. You're going to make me come too soon."

Her words made him freeze, and although still buried to the hilt inside her, they also took the edge off his own incipient orgasm.

"Isn't that a good thing?" he asked, looking down into her brown eyes, now dark with the same lust burning through his body.

She chuckled, then licked her full lips, making him want to kiss her until she gave another one of those pleasure-drunk groans.

"Orgasms are always better when delayed," she said, her deep, sexy tone making him shiver in reaction.

It was then he recognized how she'd controlled the way he touched her, and the length of time he'd stimulated the various parts of her body. While he'd been intent of giving her that ultimate pleasure, she'd been holding it off, turned on not just by what he was doing, but also by gratification deferred.

"Why didn't you say so before?" he asked, his body reacting in a way he hadn't expected, hardening even more, excited by the prospect of teasing her over and over again. So much so that he eased away from her, feeling only a small pang of regret as they uncoupled. "Let me..."

He flipped her over onto her stomach and was rewarded by another gust of delighted laughter, which quickly turned into murmurs and sighs of incipient ecstasy...

Massimo forcefully pushed the memories away, but not before his blood started to heat the way it had every time he'd thought about her, or been in her presence. The woman on Spiaggia Tordigliano, with her dark honey skin and striking brown eyes, had given as much pleasure as he'd tried to give her, but his reactions to her meant nothing.

Nothing.

And the night they'd spent together in Positano meant even less.

It was just the sort of encounter he felt comfortable having, and perhaps would seek out again in the future.

Little better than anonymous. No confidences shared. No baring of souls. Only an intense physical attraction brought to logical—explosive—conclusion.

While his mind kept turning to that wondrous night, and his body refused to let him truly rest because of the memory, it was perfect just the way things ended.

She'd moved on, and he was exactly where he was meant to be. Where he was happiest.

"Did you see the email about the new nurse while you were on vacation?" As he expected, Fatima had moved on to a completely different subject without waiting for a response. "Will you be at the welcome get-together later?"

"No."

He'd gone no-contact from work during his two-week vacation, and didn't have time for office parties. Just the thought of standing around while everyone made small talk around him was distasteful. Besides, now that Nonna had taken in a foster child, she needed his help more than ever.

Pietro was still getting used to being a part of a household, rather than one of a hundred children in a home for orphans and abandoned children. He needed a certain level of continuity, which had been disrupted when Massimo went on vacation.

"Mrs. Ricci has rented her a room for the five months she'll be here," Fatima continued, which actually surprised Massimo enough that he looked up. The nurse nodded, as though he'd asked a question. "Her *pensione* needs repairs, and she couldn't afford them, so she can't rent out rooms to tourists this year. Her son has promised to send her money from America to get the work started, but that hasn't happened yet."

It had been a lean couple of years on the Amalfi Coast for anyone involved in the tourist trade, so Massimo wasn't too surprised to hear that, although it did make him sad. Nonna had the same problem but, luckily for her, she had Massimo on hand to help her keep things afloat. Mrs. Ricci's roof had been damaged during the bad storm they'd had the year before, and it was a shame she hadn't gotten it repaired, but not surprising. Renting rooms to tourists had been her main source of income. No tourists equaled no money.

When he considered it that way, it made sense that she'd rent out a room to an itinerate worker, just to try to make ends meet.

"Are you all finished cleaning?" he asked Fatima, as he reached for the patient list she'd put on the small desk.

"Yes," she replied, pulling at the roll of paper affixed to the end of the examination table, and spreading the resulting sheet out with a flourish. "I believe it's Mrs. Giordano, next. I hope you're feeling in good voice. She seems to get deafer each time she comes in."

Massimo couldn't help smiling at that statement. It was all too true. Sometimes, between Mrs. Giordano's bellowing and his own, by the time the examination was over he felt as though his ears were ringing.

He was still smiling when he got to the door and, opening it, urged Fatima to precede him through with a slight touch on her shoulder.

Then he heard a sound that froze him in place.

A woman's laugh; as rich and deep and sweet as limoncello.

A sound he knew well. Even intimately. One he'd heard as they walked along the beach at Positano. Then again after they'd kissed for the first time and, most thrillingly, heard frequently as he and Kendra rolled about in bed, seeking and finding the ultimate delight in each other's bodies.

He'd never been with a woman who'd so frankly shown her pleasure when it came to sex. Whose unfettered joy and unrestrained search for her own unique brand of ecstasy seemed as natural as the sunrise, or a storm rushing in from the sea. And the audible evidence of her joy added another level to his own desire, elevating it to previously unknown heights, so the climb to orgasm was as thrilling as the moment of culmination.

But it couldn't be her, could it?

Feeling like a child, Massimo edged into the doorway to peer around the doorjamb. Then he drew back quickly, his body, which had already been humming as though electrified, suddenly ablaze.

It *was* her, walking with the clinic coordinator, Alessio Pisano, who was looking at Kendra as though she were a *torta caprese* and he had a taste for that decadent chocolate treat. Massimo ground his teeth, annoyed at the smarmy expression on the older man's face, and then forced himself to relax.

Encountering Kendra was inevitable, and while he wondered what she was doing here—whether she was ill and seeking treatment, or had some other reason to be at the clinic—he at least was forewarned.

Her reaction to seeing him would be interesting to behold.

So he stepped out into the corridor as though nothing at all was amiss, straight into Kendra and Alessio's path. When he made eye contact with Kendra, he knew the exact moment she recognized him by the way her eyes widened, and her lips parted in shock.

"Kendra," he said, still keeping his gaze locked on hers. "What a surprise."

She didn't reply. Instead, Alessio was the one who said, "Massimo, you've already met our new nurse?"

"Our new *nurse*?" Well, that was enough to

stop him cold, and he saw her expression change to devilish amusement, just before her chuckles rolled over him like a capricious wave.

"Yes, our new nurse. Who did you think she was? And where do you two know each other from?"

Gathering himself, trying to ignore the way his heart once more raced and sweat gathered along his spine, Massimo replied, "I was at Spiaggia Tordigliano when she saved a man from drowning."

"And the doctor performed CPR," Kendra tacked on, the amusement in her voice patently clear. "It was a brief encounter."

"But memorable," Massimo countered, unable to resist the double entendre. Letting her know, no matter how she classified what had happened between them in Positano, he hadn't forgotten even a second of it.

"Of course it would be memorable," Alessio said, with another of his smarmy smiles aimed at Kendra. "Saving a drowning man? How did you know what to do?"

"It was part of my training when I was with the Canadian Armed Forces," she replied, her smile still in place, but a slightly cooler edge to her voice. "It's not an instinct one ever forgets."

"Ah, yes, of course." Alessio beamed, and clapped his hands, as though in approbation.

"Your military training was one of the reasons the directors decided to hire you. That and your command of several languages. As I'm sure you're aware, we get a variety of tourists of different nationalities visiting the area, and the summer months are extremely busy for us as we care for them, as well as the locals."

Just then Massimo heard Fatima coming back with Mrs. Giordano. Or rather, heard Mrs. Giordano coming, as the elderly lady's shouting couldn't be missed.

"Who am I seeing today? Dr. Bianchi, or Dr. Mancini?"

"Dr. Bianchi," Fatima bellowed back.

"Oh, yes. That nice unmarried one. I like him. I keep telling my niece about him, and saying she should come to the clinic and meet him, but she won't listen to me. These young people don't know good advice when they hear it."

Massimo didn't think he'd ever blushed in his life until that moment, and it wasn't the type of sensation he relished, at all. Heat gathered in his chest and then flooded up into his face until even his ears felt as though they might spontaneously combust.

Kendra bit her bottom lip, unholy glee lighting her eyes. Leaning closer to him, she stage-whispered, "Let us not speak of this again, *sì*?"

"Concordato," he mumbled, still embarrassed, but now fighting the urge to laugh along with her.

Her amusement was infinitely appealing.

Yet he also heard the subtext of her words— the injunction that they not speak of their prior meeting again either. That they forget the night they'd spent in his hotel room, driving each other insane until the early hours of the morning.

Hopefully he'd be able to go along with her demand, and will his body to ignore her presence far better than it had just now, when all he wanted was to demand another round of passion.

"Dr. Bianchi. We're ready for you."

At Fatima's words, he excused himself and, with one last glance at Kendra's twinkling eyes, went off to deal with his patient.

CHAPTER FOUR

KENDRA STOOD AT the window of her room in Mrs. Ricci's *pensione* with her cell phone at her ear. It was just gone six thirty in the morning, and she was catching up with her cousin Koko who lived in Toronto. They tried to speak at least once every few months, and it wasn't always easy to set up a time convenient for both of them. But Koko was a DJ, and sometimes, like now, she'd call between sets. Although Kendra could hear the bass pumping, Koko must have found a relatively quiet place, because her voice came through clearly.

"So, besides the fact that the roof of your room leaks, how else has it been?"

It had been two months since they'd last spoken, when Kendra was getting ready to leave Naples and travel on to Minori. In between they'd texted, just to check in, which usually meant short messages like: Made it to Positano safely, or, You should have seen the club last night. It was jumping.

If either had anything important but not urgent to say, they saved it for their phone conversations.

"Well…" She stretched the word out, knowing Koko would be all ears. "It's been good. I've met some fun locals to hang out with, and the people at the clinic have been great. Even the doctor I slept with before I knew he was going to be a coworker."

"What?" Koko shrieked so loudly she completely drowned out the bass line behind her. "You slept with some random dude, only to find out you'd be working with him afterward?"

Kendra couldn't help laughing. "Right? Seeing him at the clinic was an awkward moment, to say the least."

"Spill. I want to know everything."

As she filled her cousin in about the near drowning at the beach, and the subsequent tryst in Positano, Kendra left out some of the juicer bits. Like the way Massimo had made her body hum, lighting her afire in a way she hadn't really expected. She was no innocent, but it was difficult to get past the memories of the night they'd spent together because it had, in a strange way, felt like an awakening of sorts.

He was the first man who'd seemed to instinctively understand that she wasn't the type to chase orgasms, as though they were the only prize available during sex. Instead, Massimo had embraced her desires, taking her close to orgasm, then letting the impulse wane just enough to keep her constantly—ecstatically—on the brink. And she'd had the chance to learn his body in intimate detail, with no holds barred. Together they'd lit the night afire, and the memories of his hoarse cries of pleasure still echoed in her head, whenever she gave them the chance to creep in.

But she didn't tell Koko any of that. After all, her cousin was always inclined to make more out of a situation than was warranted.

Instead, she told her about the shock of seeing Massimo at the clinic—her instinctive hope that he was just passing through, and sinking feeling when she realized they'd be working together.

"It was so cute," she finished up, after telling a hysterically laughing Koko about Mrs. Giordano's comments. "He blushed. Like went bright red. He looked mortified, and it took everything I had not to tease him even more."

"So," Koko asked, after she'd gotten a hold of herself. "It sounds like you had a *great* time with him. Are you still sleeping together?"

Kendra laughed.

"Nope," she said, making her voice firm and sure, even though it meant ignoring a pang of regret. Massimo really knew his way around a woman's body, and there were times she'd found herself watching him with the kind of deep hunger she couldn't deny but also couldn't afford. "You know I avoid those kinds of complications."

Koko was quiet for a second, and when she next spoke, she sounded as though she wasn't sure she should say what she was going to. "You laugh, like you always do when things aren't easy and straightforward, but not all complications are bad, Kendra."

Kendra made a rude noise. "Girl, you know I always have one foot out the door, wherever I am. That's a recipe for disaster with most men. It starts out casual and the next thing I know he's asking me if I don't want to stay." When Koko didn't reply, Kendra went for the ultimate excuse. "Besides, we work together. It would just make things…"

"Complicated?" Koko's voice was softer. "Yeah, you mentioned your aversion to complications. But most of life is a series of complications. It's just how it is."

"Not for me," she replied, putting all the conviction she could muster into her voice, lightening the conversation with her amusement, although it felt forced. "The biggest difficulty I want is deciding where I'm going next. Or having a flight canceled unexpectedly."

Koko snorted. "Okay. Okay. I hear you."

Then her cousin changed the subject, instead bringing Kendra up to speed on other family members' lives, passing on any tidbits of family gossip.

"Have you decided where you're going next?" Koko asked, near the end of their conversation.

"Not yet," Kendra said, and her heart gave a hard thump at the question. "I'm thinking I'd like to travel around Italy a bit more, before moving on. Then I'll find somewhere warm to spend winter, but I have time to decide."

And Koko seemed satisfied with that.

By the time they'd said their goodbyes and hung up, sunlight was spilling over into the narrow roadway—little better than a cobblestone path—outside the window. When Kendra had first arrived at the *pensione* she'd seen a cavalcade of donkeys passing by on their way to a construction site just up the hill, panniers on their backs filled with building materials. It had amazed her, but once she considered how narrow and steep the streets were, it made more sense. The donkeys even easily navigated the stone stairways in other parts of town, taking materials and equipment up and bringing rubble back down, the way it had been done for centuries.

Koko's question came back to her then, along with the strange sensation Kendra felt whenever she thought about leaving the Amalfi Coast. There was a timelessness to Minori that somehow soothed her soul. On her first day off she'd walked the Sentiero dei Limoni—the Lemon Trail—from Minori to Maiori, and the views and quietude had given her more peace than she'd felt for a long time. Somehow, it was a though her father walked with her, and instead of grief at his loss she'd felt contented.

And that sensation had persisted wherever she went along the coast.

In some ways it was frightening.

She was always interested in learning about the areas she visited and the locals she encountered, but something about this particular part of Italy threatened to take hold of her heart, and never let go.

Places didn't usually affect her this way. Even the people she met were viewed as transient in her life, only a select few gaining the appellation "friend." Moving on had never been difficult and in fact was something she looked forward to, but she wasn't sure it was going to be that easy leaving here.

However, that wasn't something she had to think about for a while yet, especially since she didn't always plan her adventures in advance. Her contract was from June until the end of October, which not only allowed the clinic to have coverage during the busy season, but also let the other nurses get some time off.

And, she reminded herself, for probably the

two-hundredth time over the last weeks, just because Dr. Massimo Bianchi did funny things to her insides whenever she saw him was no reason to act on the attraction. In fact, considering all the other feelings she had about Minori and its surroundings, she was better off pushing that particular complication aside!

Yet, it had been a long, fraught couple of months. Each time their eyes met, she had to fight off the memories of being in his arms. Of the way he'd touched her—both tenderly and roughly, the juxtaposition more arousing than anything she'd felt before—and the intensity of the pleasure he'd given.

"Why didn't you say so before?" he asked, and before she could reply he'd levered himself up onto his knees and away, so that their bodies separated, leaving her strangely hollow. "Let me..."

Before she knew what he planned, he grabbed her and flipped her over onto her stomach, the movement highlighting his strength. Maybe it should be scary to have a man manipulate her body so easily but, instead, it heightened her arousal.

And when he lay over her, keeping her immobilized by his weight, and began a leisurely trip down her body, all she could do was laugh, and moan, and sigh. From neck to feet, his hands and lips and tongue swept and dipped, finding new erogenous zones, taking her to the edge of orgasm before moving on, leaving her shaking with the need to come...

And now, when his hair flopped over one eye, she wanted to smooth it back, and feel it crisply curl around her fingers again.

He turned her over again after what felt like an ecstatic eternity, and looked down at her with that hot, hooded gaze.

"I'm ready now," she said, having to force the words out from a throat tight with need.

Massimo shook his head.

"I don't think so." It looked as though he was trying to smile, but it was more of a baring of his teeth. "You like anticipation, and I'm finding I like it too."

Then, before she could respond, his head was between her thighs, but his gaze stayed locked on hers, as he once more explored her with his tongue. Oh, and he knew what he was doing, stimulating every nerve ending but the ones that would take her over the edge.

Reaching down, she twisted her fingers into his hair, tugging—hard. All that did was make him chuckle, the vibrations firing into her flesh, almost undoing all the hard work he put in, causing her to arch and cry out...

If she walked up behind him at the clinic, she had to fight the urge to run her fingers down the deep hollow over his spine, knowing it was, for him, an erogenous zone.

Halfway through the night they found themselves taking a break, both sipping from bottles of water from the hotel fridge. Massimo was sitting on the edge of the bed, while Kendra reclined against the headboard, and it gave her the opportunity to fully appreciate the width and musculature of his back. He really was marvelously built, and the sight before her once more awakened the desire he'd only just satiated.

Without thought, she ran a cold, damp finger down his back, and the resulting shudder and goose bumps firing over his skin were inspiring.

"You liked that," she said, stretching to put down the water bottle on the bedside table.

"I did," he admitted, seemingly about to change position.

Her hand on his shoulder stopped him, and he looked over at her, his eyebrows rising in question.

"Stay there." She moved behind him, kneeling so she could snake her tongue around his ear, which earned her another hard shudder, and a growl. "I want to..."

Then she showed him exactly how she, too, could find ways to let anticipation build. Taking her time, she traced each muscle with her mouth, while she ran her fingers along the dip over his spine again and again, until his breath came hard and fast from between his lips. Stimulating him, until she knew he was on the brink, the way she'd been for most of the night.

The difference, though, came when she reached around his body and took his erection in hand, and didn't stop even when he told her if she didn't, he'd explode.

The way he allowed her free rein over his body was an aphrodisiac…

And those lips that she'd once thought too thin to be attractive…

Kendra shivered, her body afire with the memories, and the rampaging desire.

"Wow, Kendra. No," she said aloud, hoping to diminish the waves of lust now pulsing through her body. "This is not how we want to start the day."

Especially when in a very short time she'd be back in close proximity with Massimo.

No, getting all worked up like this wouldn't do. At all.

Massimo was in a foul mood, and he had no one to blame for that but himself.

His life—which had seemed so very perfect just months before—seemed to be going to hell in a handbasket, and he wasn't sure what to do about it.

Nonna was irritable since a couple of bookings had been canceled, and she was worried about the loss of income. Pointing out that the villas were almost fully booked from now until the end of the season didn't seem to lessen her anxiety.

Perhaps sensing her tension, Pietro retreated into silence at the slightest incident, hardly speaking at all, and only when pressed. Although the young boy did everything he was supposed to and never was rude, having him shut down that way was worrying.

And then there was Kendra Johnson...

The nurse had been nothing but pleasant and cheerful. She got on well with staff and patients alike, and treated Massimo with professional courtesy, mixed with her habitual amusement.

Yet, just seeing her put him on high alert. Hearing her laughter sent almost unbearable longing through his body.

And she expressed her amusement a lot, each deep peal bringing back those excruciatingly sensual memories.

She'd laughed breathlessly when he found a particularly sensitive spot on her body, when he asked if she liked what he was doing. Even through her eventual orgasms.

No wonder then that each time he heard that joyous sound at work, every hair on his body rose, and heat inundated his veins. How he's stopped himself from dragging her off into an examination room and ravishing her, he really didn't know.

There'd been no discussion between them, but simply a tacit agreement that they would not talk about their night of passion, nor would it be repeated.

Whereas in Positano she'd made her interest crystal clear, now she was equally clear about keeping her distance. It was maddening, since the more reticent she was, the more he wanted to know about her. Thank goodness for the village *nonne*, who didn't hesitate to ask all the questions he wanted to, and Kendra seemed quite willing to answer.

"Is it true...?" is how most of their queries started, showing that the village grapevine was working.

"Is it true you're Canadian?"

"...that you were in the army?"

"...that you speak five languages?"

As it turned out, the answer was yes to them all except the last one, where it turned out she spoke six languages, with a smattering of a few others.

One *nonna* went so far as to take Kendra's face between her palms and, after a long, searching look, said, "I did not know there were Black people in Canada. Did your family go there from somewhere else?"

He'd expected her to pull away from such an invasion of her space, but, instead, she'd stayed absolutely still, looking into Mrs. De Luca's eyes.

"There are all kinds of people in Canada, but my father's ancestor fought for the British during the American War of Independence and earned his freedom from slavery. When it was over, in 1776, he and his family were resettled in Nova Scotia, on Canada's east coast, and some of their descendants have been there ever since."

As though somehow mesmerized, Mrs. De Luca didn't release Kendra's cheeks, but asked, "And where is your mother's family from?"

That was when Kendra gently pulled away and, although she was still smiling, her tone was a little cooler as she replied, "My mother was from Argentina."

Then she changed the subject, bringing the appointment back on track.

He'd noticed she did that sometimes—smiled and shut people down at the same time. It was subtle, but once you knew what to look for, it became obvious. There were some subjects that touched a nerve, and although she didn't overtly react, there were tiny signs she threw up that said, "Step back!"

"Porca miseria," he muttered to himself, realizing he'd just wasted fifteen minutes staring

at the patient list, thinking about a woman who had no interest in him.

Kendra Johnson was so bright, so incandescent, she'd never consider a boring, laconic man like him for anything more than a spontaneous one-night stand. All he could hope was that she didn't regret their encounter, but could think back on it with some pleasure.

And, if their disparate personalities weren't enough of an impediment, there was the fact that she was the kind of woman he doubted would ever settle down in one place. A vagabond, as she herself had said.

Massimo knew he'd never be completely happy away from where he was—here on the Amalfi Coast. Perhaps that made him stodgy—an old man, as Therese had accused—but he was content with his life.

At least, he usually was.

Getting up from the desk, he made his way out to the reception area, determined to keep his mind firmly on his job, and nothing else. Of course, as soon as he opened the office door, he heard Kendra chuckle, and every muscle in his body tightened. Which meant he was scowling when he reached his destination.

"Fatima. I've been asked to make a house call to Mrs. Lionetti this evening. Are you available to accompany me?"

Giving him a somewhat startled look, which told him he was being even curter than usual, Fatima shook her head.

"No, Dr. Bianchi, I'm sorry. I have to take Marina to Salerno to meet with the ophthalmologist right after work."

Marina, Fatima's youngest daughter, had strabismus that was resistant to nonsurgical intervention.

"I can go with you, if you need a nurse," Kendra interjected.

It was on the tip of his tongue to say it wasn't necessary, and he'd go by himself, but it was clinic policy that no doctor do a nonemergency house call alone. Biting back a snort of annoyance, he nodded.

"Fine. Be ready to leave at four thirty, please. Fatima, if you'd give Kendra the file so she's aware of Mrs. Lionetti's situation, I'd appreciate it."

Then, caught somewhere between anger and anticipation, he strode back to his office, trying his best not to stomp like a petulant child as he went.

And when he heard that bedeviling laugh again, he couldn't help the little groan that rose in his throat.

She was going to make him insane, if he didn't get his reactions under control!

CHAPTER FIVE

Mrs. Lionetti was diabetic and blind, and had limited mobility because of nerve damage in her feet, which was why she was one of the patients who always had the doctor go to her.

She also happened to live on the same street where Kendra was staying, just a little lower down, but when Kendra pointed that out, all Massimo said was, "I know."

His grumpy demeanor was beginning to grate, but, at the same time, she wasn't willing to delve into why he was behaving that way. Maybe it had something to do with her, or maybe it didn't.

There was definitely a part of her that hoped it was because he was still attracted to her, but also was unwilling to do anything about it. After all, misery did love company, and this constant hum beneath her skin whenever they were together was driving her bonkers.

So, as she always did when in any way unsure, she chuckled and said, "I don't think I've been as closely monitored as I am here since I left Nova

Scotia when I was ten. Everyone seems to know my business."

That gained her a sideways glance, just short of a glare, which she proceeded to ignore. If he was going to be unpleasant the entire time, she wasn't going to jolly him along. That wasn't her way.

Even though, for once, she felt as though she wanted to.

Mrs. Lionetti was frail and querulous. Even when her son Tino told her who was at the door, she kept fussing.

"It's not time for me to see the doctor again. He was just here the other day."

"Ah, Mrs. Lionetti." Massimo's voice was soft, cajoling. "Didn't you miss me? It's been months since we saw each other."

"No, it hasn't, young man." Mrs. Lionetti's chin lifted belligerently. "You were here just a few days ago. And who is that with you?"

"This is Nurse Kendra Johnson."

"That strange foreign woman everyone has been talking about? Who likes to gad about at all hours of night? Going to the *taverna* and encouraging other young women into disreputable ways?"

Kendra had to bite her lip not to laugh. With a feisty matriarch like this, it would definitely set the wrong tone. And it didn't bother her in the slightest that her efforts to befriend the locals and enjoy her time in Minori were being classified in such a way. She'd developed a little cadre of ladies she usually had dinner with, and then they stopped off at one of the *tavernas* afterward. No doubt her being in the restaurants and bars late into the evening was seen as somehow questionable, despite being in the company of local acquaintances.

Ignoring the curious looks the two men were giving her, she said, "That's me, Mrs. Lionetti."

The elderly lady's eyebrows went up, and she gave a little snort, but said, "Well, come closer and tell me why you're here. I want to know who you are."

Kendra intercepted a glance from Massimo, who indicated he would be going into the adjacent room to speak to Mrs. Lionetti's son, and she nodded in understanding. No doubt Massimo wanted to ask Tino about his mother's memory lapses, if that was what they were.

So, Kendra submitted to the third degree while taking the other woman's blood pressure and pulse, and listening to both chest and abdominal sounds. When Massimo came back into the room, she handed him the chart with her notations, and stepped back so he could begin his own examination.

From some of his questions, Kendra thought he might suspect Mrs. Lionetti of having a UTI, which could account for her confusion, but there were also other diseases and syndromes to consider. Non-24-hour sleep-wake disorder was one, since sufferers of blindness who tried to adhere to a normal schedule when their circadian rhythm was disrupted often exhibited signs of depression, and sometimes confusion. Insulin resistance in the brain or a small stroke were also possibilities.

Hopefully it wasn't irreversible dementia, or the onset of Alzheimer's disease, but she had no doubt Massimo would test for those too.

He was getting to the end of his examination when there was a huge, rumbling crash from outside, followed by a series of shouts and screams. Without thought, Kendra was on her feet and out the front door, looking first right and then left. To the left, farther up the hill, near Mrs. Ricci's house, she could see a cloud of dust, and some figures milling around, so she ran that way.

Then she came to a halt, staring for a moment at the devastation before her.

There was a pile of rubble almost filling the narrow street, right in front of Mrs. Ricci's house, and what was left of a house across the road from the *pensione* where Kendra boarded. Then she realized a group of men were frantically digging at the debris with their bare hands, tossing rocks away.

Running up to them, Kendra shouted, to be heard above the hubbub, "What happened?"

"Part of a building has collapsed. There's a man under here, somewhere."

She didn't hesitate, but set to work, grabbing pieces of stone, wood and other detritus, joining the effort to free the trapped worker.

"Guarda! Guarda!"

In the instant it took her to realize what the man next to her was saying, she heard a roar, as the pile shifted, beginning to collapse with an ugly groan, like a dying beast.

Before she could do more than take a step, someone grabbed her around the waist and swung her around, just as a building across from the original one damaged partially collapsed right onto where she'd been standing. Her rescuer hadn't been quite quick enough, as she felt a hard blow to her left arm.

A dust cloud descended over them, particles getting into her eyes making her tear ducts work overtime, and causing both her and her rescuer to cough.

It was only when she heard Massimo's voice, asking if she were all right, that she realized it was him, and that he had her securely—safely—held tight against his chest.

"Yes," she managed to say, between coughing fits. "But we need to get back and help the worker."

"*Sì.*" But he was running his hands over her arms and back, as though checking for injuries, and it took everything she had not to gasp when he touched that tender spot on her outer bicep. "But that was too close for comfort. If I asked you to stay back, would you comply?"

Normally, she would have laughed, and told him no way, but even with his face covered in dust and sweat, she could see the concern in his expression, and her heart clenched.

"Thank you for asking," she said, forcing herself to ease out of his arms, and shaking her head. "But no."

"*Eccolo! Eccolo!* I see him! Here! Here!"

And they were rushing back to the point where the injured man had been discovered, Massimo shouting orders, trying to tell the others not to move him, to be careful they didn't cause the pile to shift again.

"My bag," he snapped in her direction, and Kendra took off back to Mrs. Lionetti's house.

The elderly lady was clutching her sweater closed at the base of her throat, her eyes wide and her lips trembling as she called out, "What has happened? Where is Tino?"

"He'll be right back, Mrs. Lionetti," Kendra said, as she grabbed Massimo's stethoscope, and picked up his medical bag. "There's been an accident up the hill, but Tino's okay."

She hoped that was the truth. She hadn't recalled seeing the other man at the scene, but that wasn't surprising.

It was just total chaos.

Sprinting back, she found Massimo and two other men clearing additional rubble away from the patient.

Focusing on helping Massimo, she watched him check the man's vitals, while she found a neck brace, having it to hand when he needed it. Her arm was throbbing, but a quick look assured her there was no cut, as the light sweater she was wearing over her scrubs didn't appear to be torn, and there was no sign of blood.

"Concussion, and fracture of right radius and ulna," Massimo said, glancing up at the pile of rubble, which although now diminished still loomed above them in a menacing way. "No way to gauge spinal damage or internal injuries here. I'd rather not move him until we can get him on a back board."

"There's one at the clinic," she said. "Should I go get it?"

It would take her less than ten minutes to get there and back.

He shook his head, and she realized why when

she heard, faintly in the distance, the wail of approaching sirens.

"The paramedics will soon be here. You should step back now. There's nothing more you can do."

She ignored him. The injured man had a free-bleeding laceration on his head and she'd already prepared a gauze pad to put on it. Applying pressure to the wound, she spared Massimo a glance, and found him giving her a glare.

"Guarda!" one of the men nearby shouted, causing Kendra to think the pile was shifting again and throw herself forward, trying to protect the patient. "Crazy woman! Get away from there!"

Realizing there was something else going on, she looked up, but it took her a few long moments to understand what she was seeing.

"That's Mrs. Ricci," she said, recognizing the older woman, who was standing looking out of a hole that had been punched in the side of a house. "What is she doing there? And why is she crying? Is this a relative of hers?"

"No," Massimo said. "The building collapsed right onto her house, and damaged it too."

It took a moment for that to sink in, then Kendra couldn't hold back the curse that issued from her mouth. "And that's my room in her house."

She didn't understand the sound Massimo made, until she looked at him and realized he looked—incongruously—as though he was battling both sympathy and amusement. Then she understood why as he dipped his head, drawing her attention toward a bright bit of lacy cotton sticking out between the rubble.

"I think that may be yours too."

She cursed again, wondering just how much of her clothes, especially her underwear, were buried under the pile.

And she could have smacked Massimo right there, in front of everyone, as he clearly struggled not to laugh.

Luckily for him, the ambulance attendants arrived just then, and she was forced to move out of their way.

Massimo made his report to the paramedics and assisted them to stabilize the patient for transport, before getting up and looking around for Kendra.

Now that the immediate danger was past, he was surprised at the anger pulsing through him.

He'd forever remember the moment when he'd seen the pile of rocks and debris tilt, sickeningly, above her while she remained unaware, having not immediately understood the shouted warning.

If anyone had told him he could move as fast as he had then, he wouldn't have believed them, but somehow he'd reached her side and yanked her away.

Even after that, when he asked her to move to a safe distance, she'd refused, splitting his attention between her and his patient. It had enraged him, even as he knew there was nothing he could do about it.

Now, she'd apparently disappeared, leaving him with no outlet for his anger.

"Massimo." He turned to find Roberto "Rosso" Gallo standing at his shoulder, staring at the devastation. Rosso was a local builder and businessman, and he was shaking his head. "I warned them this would happen if they didn't repair the damage caused to the foundation by the storm last summer, but they wouldn't listen."

"They didn't hire you to fix it, then?"

Rosso shook his head. "The owner of the house said I was too expensive, and I heard he'd given his cousin the job." He shrugged. "Instead of fixing the foundation, when I passed by last month, I saw they'd put on another room on top of the house. It looks like the foundation couldn't take the weight."

Massimo caught a glimpse of Kendra, who was hugging a crying Mrs. Ricci. Excusing himself, he walked over to them, just in time to hear one of the men standing beside them say, "No, no. You can't go back in there. It might not be safe."

"I have to." Kendra's voice was firm. "Everything I own is in that room. At least, whatever is left that isn't scattered down here."

"And if you fall to your death, what good will that do?"

Kendra shrugged. "Well, I won't need my stuff then, will I?"

His heart all but stopped. He was beginning to recognize the deep vein of independence that ran through this infuriating, crazy woman, and he wondered if he'd have to cart her away over his shoulder to stop her doing something stupid.

As though hearing his thoughts, she sent him a steely glare.

"Don't you start on me, Massimo." She said it in English and her voice wobbled slightly. In that moment, he realized that the fright was setting in, as the adrenaline in her system waned. "My passport, everything is in there, and I'm going in to get them."

It came to him, right then and there, that he couldn't let her do it, and there was only one way to stop her.

Turning away, he swiftly climbed the pile nearest the entrance to Mrs. Ricci's home and down the other side, glad to see the doorway was clear enough for him to make it through. Behind him came shouts, including from Kendra, but it was, he reasoned, already too late anyway, since he was partway up the stairs.

Judging from the configuration of the house in comparison with the street, it took him only a moment to find her room, and then he hesitated at the doorway. Even from there he could see how the floor sagged toward the broken wall, and, as though in warning, the house creaked, moaning as if in pain.

No time to lose courage now though.

Looking around, he spotted a battered knapsack at the foot of the bed, and a small duffel bag on the floor, close to a now dust-covered dressing table. There were a few bottles and tubes on the tabletop too, so, taking a deep breath, he made his way cautiously toward it. Again, shouts and screams came from below as he came into view from the street, but he ignored them as he grabbed the duffel, unzipped it and swept the bottles and tubes into it.

Then he swiftly pulled open the drawers and scooped their contents into it too.

The floor creaked. Something beneath his feet broke with a snap, and Massimo knew he'd tested his luck as far as he should.

Making his way as quickly as he could to the door, he snagged the knapsack on his way past, then a tablet from the nightstand, stuffing it into the duffel, and made it out into the small corridor.

It was only when he made it back down to the

front door that he realized he'd been holding his breath almost the entire time.

There were men standing on the rubble, and they gave a shout of satisfaction when he appeared, and the assembled crowd cheered as he passed the bags across, and then climbed back to safety.

All except the woman he'd done it all for.

As he approached, she hauled back a bunched fist. Luckily, he leaned away, avoiding the punch she aimed squarely at his chest. *Dio* only knew how much damage she would have done had it landed. At the same time she was shouting, "You idiot! You nincompoop! What the hell were you thinking?"

And, as everyone else stood there in shocked silence, and Kendra glared at him as though she wanted to murder him, Massimo found himself rubbing his chest, as though her blow had actually struck home, trying his best not to burst out laughing.

Her eyes narrowed, and her beautiful lips firmed into a straight, angry line. "Don't you dare laugh, Massimo Bianchi. Don't you dare!"

"But you are so very beautiful when you are angry," he said, saying the first thing that came to mind. "How else am I to respond but with joy and jubilation?"

Once more the men within earshot cheered and

laughed, while Kendra threw her hands in the air in obvious disgust, grabbed her bags from the ground and walked away.

But it was too late.

Massimo had seen the devilish twinkle in her eyes, and knew he was already forgiven, for everything.

CHAPTER SIX

KENDRA TRIED TO stay furious at Massimo. Oh, she did her very best. Ignoring him while they gave their reports to the *polizia*. Giving him frosty yes-or-no answers when he asked her questions. Going off—pointedly alone—while she tried to figure out where on earth she was going to go, since her place of residence had been declared unsafe. Even glaring at him while he, so infuriatingly calm, suggested that she come back with him to his grandmother's *agriturismo*.

"She has space, so it won't be a problem. Then you don't have to worry about where you're going to stay until tomorrow."

She really wanted to tell him to go to hell, but somehow all she could remember was the sight of him climbing over the rubble, going to get her belongings, and most of her anger drained away. Then she recalled his saying she was beautiful, and the rest melted into nothing.

With a sigh of resignation, she agreed.

But when they were finally getting into his

car where he'd left it by the clinic, she knew she couldn't just let it go.

"What you did earlier was incredibly stupid, Massimo. You could have been killed." Slamming her door for emphasis, she turned sideways in her seat, so she was looking at him, as she buckled her seat belt. "Did you hear the inspector say he was surprised the floor of that room hadn't come down when the other building hit Mrs. Ricci's house?"

He sent her a sideways glance, and his lips twitched. Kendra wasn't sure whether he was annoyed or holding back a smile.

"You were planning to go in there."

Kendra growled, which earned her a lifted eyebrow. "It was my stuff. And I'm lighter than you are. There would have been much less danger." When he didn't reply, she added, "Besides, think about it logically. You're one of three doctors serving two communities. You're far more important than an itinerate nurse."

"I disagree. And I'm sure your family would too."

Would they?

She didn't say it, but the thought sat heavily in her mind. The only member of her family she was close to was Koko. Even her aunt Raylene, Koko's mother, hardly ever reached out, although Kendra had lived with her the longest of all her relatives.

It was mostly the result of the peripatetic life she'd chosen, and there was no use fussing about the fallout of it now, but the moment of sadness lingered and had to be forcefully ignored.

"Besides," Massimo continued. "It's already done. There's no need to analyze it to death at this point."

Biting back a sharp retort, Kendra decided to leave well enough alone. While the memory of the fear she'd felt at his chivalrous—no, stupid!— actions was one she knew would never fade, she was honest enough to know he was right. She had planned on going into the house herself, and she wouldn't have given a second thought to how that would make anyone else feel.

She was used to looking out for herself, and doing whatever needed to be done. She hadn't needed a knight in shining armor, but perhaps it was a tad ungrateful to kick up such a stink about, for once, having one.

As for what he'd said, about her being beautiful when she was angry—well, she wasn't touching that with a ten-foot pole.

It was all nonsense anyway, designed to stop her in her tracks and get him off the hook. While she rather hated the thought that he'd won *that* round, she had no choice but to just let it go.

As they were speaking, Massimo had been driving up into the hills above Minori, on a narrow road that first dipped into a valley and then rose again, so that the lights of the coast became distant and milky. Wishing it were daylight, so she could see the surroundings and appreciate the view, Kendra wondered just how far away his grandmother's house was. And she couldn't help hoping it had a good supply of hot water.

She stank, and was covered in dust.

Lovely way to be introduced to Massimo's family...

That thought drew her up, sharply.

It wasn't an introduction, per se. Not in the sense of there being anything between them, and her needing to make a good impression. If it could have been avoided, completely, she would have much rather do that, but it was necessity born of happenstance, and she refused to think of it in any other way.

Just to make sure he realized that too, she said, "Tomorrow I'll ask around for somewhere else to stay."

"Mmm-hmm." The alacrity of his response left no doubt that he was in full agreement. "I can make inquiries too. There are a couple of places I can think of that aren't too far from the clinic, and although the season is in full swing, they may be able to accommodate you."

"Good. Thank you."

But there was a little corner of her mind asking why it was he was so eager to get rid of her.

The car slowed, and then turned into a driveway so narrow Kendra wondered how it fit through the stone gates at all. The drive itself was short, with a dip into a swale and then back up to reveal a cobbled parking area and her first glimpse of the farmhouse.

The stone building had a square, solid look, not unlike the man beside her.

"Welcome to Agriturismo Villa Giovanna," Massimo said, and there was no mistaking the pride in his voice. "While it does not look like much now, in the dark, in the daylight it is very lovely."

"I'm sure it is." She refused to tell him that even in the gloom of night she thought it fascinating, and couldn't wait to see inside. "Is it named after your grandmother?"

"No. No. The name is much older than she is. This farm has been in my grandfather's family for many generations. There have been times when they thought they would lose it but, somehow, we never have. When my *nonno* died, my father and his siblings tried to get Nonna to sell, because they knew she wouldn't be able to manage the land on her own. But, instead, she built villas and a common room where she serves her guests breakfast. She also accommodates group tours, focusing on the food we produce, as well as leasing out some of the farmlands."

As he brought the car to a stop, Kendra replied, "And saved it once again. Are none of your father's brothers or sisters interested in farming?"

Massimo shook his head, and his lips twisted into a rueful smile. "None. And in a way, Nonna is to blame, since she insisted that all of them concentrate on their educations. She always says, though, that it's her duty to preserve Villa Giovanna and the farmland for the generations to come."

"She's hoping you, or one of your siblings or cousins, will want to take it over." Kendra could completely understand that impulse—the desire to preserve the past—although it wasn't always feasible. "Do you think one of you will?"

Massimo paused with his door partially open, and looked back at her with a smile.

"It will probably be me. This place captured my heart from I was a little boy, and I doubt it will ever let me go, fully."

Something inside her softened, and once more she thought of the Nova Scotia shore—and of her father—and she understood.

"Then you should hold on to it, just as it holds on to you."

For a moment they were connected more intimately than they had when they were naked, their bodies joined together in ecstasy, and Kendra couldn't break away from his far-too-tender gaze.

His lips opened, but what he was about to say never got uttered, as the light over the front door flashed on, and they both turned toward it.

"Massimo. Are you coming inside?"

The elderly lady standing there was nothing like Kendra expected. Considering Massimo's size and height, she'd thought perhaps his grandmother would be tall and stout. And, having heard they were a farming family, she'd assumed Mrs. Bianchi would have the careworn look she'd seen on many of the faces of the elderly women who came to the clinic. Instead, the woman peering out at them was none of those things.

Diminutive and effortlessly elegant in a flowing dress and chic sweater, Massimo's grandmother was the antithesis of everything Kendra had imagined. And even though she hadn't even gotten out of the car yet, she already felt huge and lumpish in comparison.

Not to mention filthy.

Even from a distance she was sure the older woman smelled lovely. Wildflowers, perhaps. Or some insanely expensive perfume.

"Come on and meet Nonna."

Massimo was already swinging his feet out of the car, and Kendra followed suit, somewhat reluctantly.

No amount of reminding herself she didn't care what impression she made, wasn't a guest, or even Massimo's friend, really, could totally beat back the thought that she didn't belong here. Had no right even crossing that threshold.

Getting out of the car, she grabbed her bags from the back seat, and went to catch up with Massimo, who was waiting for her at the edge of the parking area. As they approached the door, Mrs. Bianchi stepped back into the hallway beyond, and Kendra could see the worry on her face.

"Filomena called to tell me about the building falling and that you were there." Uncaring of his filthy state, she reached out and pulled Massimo close for a hug. "Were you hurt?"

Kendra stood back and watched as Massimo subjected himself to being patted and examined like a little boy, and she couldn't stop the smile spreading across her face. It was, for want of a better word, precious.

"I'm fine, Nonna. Not hurt at all." As though needing to distract her, he continued, "This is Nurse Kendra Johnson, who was staying with Mrs. Ricci. That house was damaged too, so I suggested she come and stay here tonight."

Now Kendra found herself under scrutiny, but, surprisingly, it wasn't uncomfortable. Perhaps it was because Massimo and his grandmother shared that particular way of looking at a person—searchingly, but not rudely—and now she was used to it.

When the older lady extended her hand, Kendra put down her bags and moved closer to shake it.

She'd been wrong, after all. Mrs. Bianchi didn't smell of flowers, or perfume. Instead there was the distinctive, mouthwatering scent of fresh-baked bread surrounding her, which was even better.

"Of course she can stay here. You poor girl. Is that all you were able to save from Maria's house? Will you be able to get the rest at another time?"

"No, Mrs. Bianchi. This is everything."

Well, everything except her second pair of scrubs and the two pairs of underwear that had been hanging on a drying rack next to her window, and now were buried in the rubble of Mrs. Ricci's house.

"Kendra is a seasoned adventurer, Nonna, and travels light."

"I see." She said it slowly, as though she *didn't* see, at all, but there was no judgment in her tone, just honest surprise. "Well, you are very welcome, Kendra. I hope you'll be comfortable."

"I'm sure I will."

"Is there space in one of the villas, Nonna?"

At Massimo's question, she turned what looked like a shocked face his way.

"Oh, no. She stays here, with us. I just need to make up the guest room bed."

Best to make it plain, from now, that she didn't consider herself a real guest in their home, and certainly didn't need coddling.

"If you tell me where to find the sheets, I can make the bed myself, Mrs. Bianchi. I don't want to put you out."

"Oh, but…"

"I'll take her up to the guest room, Nonna, and give her clean sheets and a blanket."

Kendra knew that no-nonsense tone quite well, and apparently so did his grandmother, as she made no further argument, just said, "Well, by the time you both get cleaned up, I'll have some supper ready for you."

A little movement at the end of the hallway caught Kendra's eye, just as Massimo asked, "Where is Pietro?"

The little boy who had been peering around the corner pulled back, as though not wanting to be seen. From clinic gossip, Kendra knew Ms. Bianchi had taken in a foster child, and she assumed the little blond boy she'd glimpsed was that child, rather than a relative.

"He's in the kitchen, doing some work I set for him, so he doesn't forget everything he learnt this year over the summer. I know he'd rather be playing, but he's being a good boy. You can introduce him to Kendra when you come back down to eat."

She saw the hesitation in the way Massimo took a step toward the staircase but his focus remained on the other end of the hallway. And then he sighed, and Kendra could swear his shoulders slumped a little.

"Yes. Of course."

He reached back, and before she realized what he was doing, had picked up her bags from the ground and was heading for the stairs.

As she hustled to catch up, she resisted the urge to grab her stuff from him, but when they got to the landing, she said, "I could have carried those."

"Of course you could," he replied in a tone so serene she wanted to smack him. "You carried them into the house all by yourself, didn't you? But Nonna would skin me alive if I had allowed it."

And there really wasn't anything much she could say to counter that.

The room Massimo showed her to was lovely. While downstairs the floors were of red, hexagonal tiles, upstairs had beautiful wooden floors and, in the guest room, colorful rugs beside the bed that matched the curtains. The furniture was obviously antique and, although rather plain, quite lovely. There was the scent of a lemony polish and a calm, soothing atmosphere to the room—in fact to all she'd seen of the house so far—and Kendra started to relax.

"I hope you don't mind sharing a bathroom with me?"

Of course, he meant it innocently enough, but her mind immediately made the leap to both of them, naked, in the shower, together. Even as exhausted as she was, that image made her entire body heat, and had tension coiling her muscles into knots.

It took swallowing, hard, and a forceful effort to keep her voice level, so as to reply, "Of course not. Will you shower first, or shall I?"

She turned toward him as she spoke, and the expression she saw on his face made her internal temperature spike into the stratosphere. Somehow, she knew without a doubt he'd had the same fantastical thought as she had, and the same instinctive reaction to it. An invitation to share the shower rose to her lips, and had to be forcefully subdued.

He cleared his throat, and spun on his heel to head for the door.

"Ladies first. I'll go and find the sheets and towels for you."

As he closed the door behind him, Kendra let out a muffled groan, and only just stopped herself from flopping her dirty self down onto the clean white bedspread.

It was going to be a long, long night.

CHAPTER SEVEN

MASSIMO CAME DOWNSTAIRS the following morning, and found only his grandmother in the kitchen, which surprised him. He'd knocked on Kendra's door when passing, to tell her he would be leaving for the clinic in half an hour, and got no response.

"Where is Kendra?" he asked, as he went to pour himself a café latte.

"She left already," Nonna replied, taking a basket of oranges and apples to the table, in a less-than-subtle hint for him to eat something healthy, rather than just one of her freshly baked pastries. "She came down about an hour ago and asked if there were any buses coming by. I offered her some breakfast, but she said because of the incident last night she needed to see to some errands in town before work, and went to catch the bus."

Massimo only just bit back the curse that rose to his lips, but stifled it with a sip of his coffee.

"She could have just waited for me," he grumbled.

Nonna chuckled, but it was a rueful sound.

"She's very independent, your Nurse Kendra. Besides, she'd not have been able to get anything done before work if she'd waited for you."

Again Massimo had to stop himself from saying what came first to his lips—that she wasn't *his* Kendra. But if he'd said it aloud, Nonna would read all kinds of things into his words.

That he didn't doubt.

The night before he'd seen her try to draw the younger woman out, with surprisingly little effect. With the candor he'd seen Kendra display in the clinic when questioned by other women, he'd thought she'd be more forthcoming. But although she'd been scrupulously polite, Nonna hadn't gotten much out of her.

Then Massimo had caught Nonna watching both him and Kendra at different times in the evening, as though trying to gauge their relationship. It had made him self-conscious, but Kendra either didn't notice or didn't care.

He'd tried to be as casual as possible but, as sometimes happened, the harder he tried, the more his brain kept turning to naughty, inappropriate thoughts. Like how earlier he'd instantly gotten hard at the thought of her in the shower, and how his damned penis was once again stirring just from that imagined picture.

Or fantasizing about her sneaking into his room later, and climbing into his bed with him.

He would never be so bold as to do any such thing himself, but Kendra… Oh, Kendra was bold enough, sassy enough, secure enough to come to his room if she wanted to.

And he wanted her to.

As if all that wasn't enough, Pietro had been completely silent after mumbling a hello when prompted. No matter what was being said, he sat there, just watching each of them in turn, not joining in the conversation.

Not that the little boy was ever voluble. On the whole he was a quiet child, with an air of attentive caution about him. Nonna believed that once he felt secure in the house—with them—he would come out of his shell, but it had been months and Massimo had seen no sign of it happening.

It made him sad, and made him also wonder if the attention he was giving Pietro was sufficient.

If he were enough of a person, of a man, to be a good role model and mentor.

He would have liked to know how to draw the little boy out, encourage him to talk more, but as a man who only spoke when necessary himself, he didn't know how. Besides, perhaps that was just Pietro's nature and trying to draw him out more would only make him unhappy. How did one determine something like that, when they had no experience with raising children?

And it was no use looking at his own strained

relationship with his father for inspiration. Papa never truly seemed to understand Massimo, or was interested in figuring him out. Instead, he'd poked fun at the son who only reluctantly participated in sports. The one who preferred to have his nose in a book than go out like his brothers did, and retreated into the background whenever possible to avoid the drama his siblings seemed to thrive on.

That had led to a certain amount of ridicule as Massimo was growing up, and even when he became a doctor, he was left with the feeling nothing he did would ever be good enough.

The only thing he knew was that wasn't how parenting should be done, but it didn't help him figure out the best way forward. As a result, Massimo found himself double- and triple-guessing his words and actions when interacting with the little boy.

"Where is Pietro?"

"He should be down soon." She glanced at her watch. "He's probably engrossed in one of his little projects, and losing track of time." Pietro liked to tinker with anything mechanical or electronic he could get his hands on. "I'll call him if it gets too late. But, before I do, I want to talk to you."

Not knowing what to expect, Massimo watched as his grandmother picked up her cup from the counter and came to sit across from him at the table.

"Okay. Is there something you need me to do?"

Nonna shook her head, and then shrugged. "Well, yes, although not in the way I think you mean. We are all set for our next guests, and you've done a wonderful job in helping me get ready, but…"

Her voice faded, and she took a sip of coffee before looking back up. By the time she did, Massimo was on pins and needles. He hated when she lost her habitual forthrightness, since it usually meant she was about to say something he didn't want to hear.

So he kept silent, watching her, until she shrugged again and said, "I think we should offer to have Nurse Kendra come and stay here."

"No." His refusal was instinctive, and foolish. Nonna's eyes narrowed in speculation, and he hurried to continue. "I don't think it would be a good idea. We are too far out of town, and she probably would prefer to be closer to the clinic."

"She's already discovered that there's a bus just down the hill," Nonna pointed out. "And you can drive her back and forth when your schedules coincide."

"Nonna, Kendra is a free spirit. I don't think she'd want to be stuck up here with us." He felt sad as he said it, and even a little silly. The villa was only a fairly short drive up from the village, and a twenty-minute walk downhill would take you right to the outskirts of Minori.

"No one is stuck here, Massimo, except perhaps you." He stared at her, annoyed and, although he hated to admit it, rather hurt too. "She can come and go as she pleases, just as you can, and if she spends time enjoying herself rather than locked away in the house, I say good for her. Perhaps she can set a good example for you, and you'll get out more yourself."

He wanted to argue, to say he was completely happy with his life, *grazie mille*, but the words stuck in his throat. Nonna wasn't saying anything he hadn't heard before, or knew to be untrue. He had turned into a hermit over the last few years, yet hadn't wanted to change that status.

The risk could be too great. The outcome too painful.

"I don't care what Kendra does."

He knew he sounded less like a grown man and more like a recalcitrant child, and when his grandmother snorted, he realized she'd heard it too.

"Then you should have no objection to her staying here."

Oh, he had all kinds of objections.

Like the fact he'd hardly slept a wink the night

before, thinking about her just there, on the other side of his bedroom wall.

And the fact that being around her made him a little *pazzo*. Tempted to lose all caution and do things he'd never considered before. Like go into half-destroyed buildings, so she wouldn't have to, or try to entice her back into his bed, even if that bed was located in his *nonna*'s home.

"Massimo. The money she will pay in rent will go a long way to help me. You know this."

One last attempt to try to make her see reason.

"The villas are almost fully booked all the way to winter. You have at least five groups coming to do cooking tours, and the restaurants are open, so the farm produce is selling again, and you won't have to give much of it away like you did the last couple of years. Isn't that enough?"

Nonna shook her head. "Every bit helps, after what we went through. We should do this."

Desperate now, he again said, "Kendra may not want to stay here."

Pushing back her chair, Nonna stood up and gave him a long, hard look.

"At least ask her, Massimo. For me."

Then she went out into the hallway to call Pietro down for breakfast, leaving Massimo staring balefully into his coffee.

Cavolo!

* * *

By the time the clinic doors opened to the patients, Kendra had achieved a lot more than she'd expected to.

Found her way down from Villa Giovanna to Minori, without having to wait for Massimo.

Got breakfast of a café latte and pastry from the harborside café that opened before dawn to serve the fishermen and other early risers.

Then, taking her breakfast to go, she'd sat in front of the laundromat, knowing it wouldn't open for at least another hour and a half, but willing to wait. After all, her one surviving pair of scrubs was filthy, and she had to get them washed. Usually she'd do her washing herself, but today she was willing to pay extra for the proprietor's wife to do it for her, so she could get to work on time. Hopefully she could borrow something to wear, other than her less-than-professional white knit pants and band T-shirt.

She'd thought about asking Massimo or his grandmother for use of their washing machine the night before, but decided against it. Sitting around the kitchen table with Massimo, his *nonna* and Pietro had felt uncomfortable, but not in a way she would ever have expected.

There was that extreme awareness she always had around Massimo—that physical yearning she was able to subdue while at work—but which now, after all they'd gone through, was changed and heightened. She knew he'd endangered himself to help her and, in his own macho way, keep her safe. It both angered her and, somehow, lowered her resistance toward him.

Last night she was forced to acknowledge he had become even more of a threat to her peace than before, and that was saying a lot.

As if dealing with that weren't enough, there was Nonna, who turned out not to be the elegant doyen Kendra had assumed her to be on sight, but a far more dangerous beast: the mothering type.

There was absolutely no doubt in Kendra's mind that if she allowed that woman a toehold into her life, there would be all kinds of smothering and taking care of going on.

And that was the last thing she needed—or wanted—right now. Probably ever.

Yeah, definitely ever.

Then there was Pietro.

Seven or eight years old she judged, from his size and the fact that his adult upper front teeth were already in, but with the watchful light blue gaze of an old, old man. The type of man who's been through hell and is waiting for the other shoe to drop.

A gaze she knew all too well, from looking into the mirror as a child.

He tugged on her heartstrings—hard. She

wanted to know what he was afraid of, here in this beautiful farmhouse, with people who obviously cared about him. Both Massimo and his grandmother made every effort to draw the little boy out, but he wouldn't budge from that cautious, disbelieving stance.

But it was clear he'd been with them for a while. There was a certain routine in how the three of them moved together.

When she'd come down from having her shower, Mrs. Bianchi had said, "There you are, right on time. Pietro just finished setting the table. Massimo never takes long in the shower, so I'll start dishing out."

And Pietro had picked up a platter from the sideboard, and taken it to the stove for Mrs. Bianchi, with the easy manner of habit. Just like when Massimo came into the room and saw dinner already on the table, he'd gone to open a bottle of wine, and poured glasses for the adults. Then, in one of the sweetest gestures ever, he'd taken a bottle out of the refrigerator and poured some of its contents into another wineglass, which he set at Pietro's place setting.

There was such a homey atmosphere in that house, she almost couldn't stand it, and it made her even more curious about what had put that fear in Pietro's eyes.

She'd gotten out of there as quickly as possible that morning, just grateful that she'd been too exhausted to stay awake all night, thinking about Massimo being just a few steps away. But she had to admit that when she'd woken up and opened the curtains, she'd wanted, oh, so badly, to go down into the terraced garden and explore its beauty.

The view had made her breath hitch, and was another reason not to linger at Villa Giovanna.

Now, sitting outside the laundromat, surfing the web, looking for a shop close by that sold medical scrubs, she felt a strange mixture of sadness and relief at her swift escape.

"Buon giorno." Kendra looked up from her phone to see a man who looked vaguely familiar smiling at her. "You're the nurse who tried to punch Dottore Massimo yesterday. Such a strong blow! It's is very good he stepped away."

When he laughed, she couldn't help laughing with him. After he'd rehashed the entire building collapse, complete with wild hand motions and sound effects, he got around to asking her why she was there. On hearing she was waiting for the laundromat to open, he called the proprietor, who turned out to be his cousin. The next thing Kendra knew, the owner's wife came down and let her in, then promptly went back upstairs to finish feeding her family, leaving Kendra alone in the store.

Surprisingly, it was easy to find a place in Salerno that sold scrubs, and she placed an order for two new pairs, having learned the hard way that having an extra was wise.

You never knew when the house you were staying in might disintegrate, taking a pair of scrubs and a couple of pairs of panties with it.

So, by nine, she'd gotten to work under her own steam, had a full belly, clean scrubs and more on the way, and had told her coworkers the entire story about the night before.

What she didn't have was a new place to stay.

She'd started texting all her new friends in Minori the evening before, and although she'd had a number of people offer temporary accommodation, that wasn't what she was looking for. She really needed somewhere she could settle into for the next few months, until she moved on again. There was nothing worse than wasting valuable time constantly having to find and move to a new spot, when she could be exploring her surroundings.

But the tourist season was already in full swing, and the boardinghouses were full of seasonal workers. Plus, none of the *pensiones* were interested in negotiating a long-term lease, since short-term rentals and high turnover brought in a lot more revenue.

Having been in the storeroom when Massimo

arrived, at least she didn't have to deal with seeing him immediately, and she wasn't scheduled to work with him either, which was a relief. She was sure he'd be annoyed that she'd left without waiting for him, or allowing his *nonna* to mollycoddle her with breakfast and more nosy questions. So, it was something of a surprise when he sent for her just as the clinic was closing for lunch, asking that she come to his office.

Already on high alert, she plastered a smile on her face before opening the door, although she didn't really feel particularly friendly. Or, to be more precise, felt perhaps too friendly toward him, as in wanting to grab him, kiss him, entice him into every naughty act they could manage.

"You wanted to see me?" she asked, standing in the open doorway, one foot in the office, the other still in the passageway.

Massimo looked up from the file he was making notes in, his expression so grim her heart faltered for a second.

"Come in, please. And close the door."

For a moment she considered refusing, but eventually did as bid. But she didn't walk any closer, staying just inside the door. He didn't ask her to sit down but, instead, rose and walked around to sit on the front edge of the desk. When he didn't immediately speak, but just sat staring at her with those unfathomable midnight eyes, her pulse rate went into overdrive. So she reacted the way she always did when feeling put on the spot.

She laughed.

His eyes flared with dark fire, and then narrowed, as she asked, "Am I in trouble or something? Maybe Nonna is upset because I ran out without breakfast?"

If the way his lips tightened meant anything, that had struck a nerve, but she ignored a pang of guilt, and kept smiling.

"She understood," he said in a low growl of a voice. "But that isn't what I want to talk to you about. *She* asked me to suggest that you rent a room from her at the villa."

The emphasis made it clear this was strictly his *nonna*'s idea, and he wasn't as enthusiastic, which made it him and her alike. Yet there was a contrary part of her that wanted to feign enthusiasm, just to tweak his tail. Subduing it—and another bubble of amusement—took more effort than she expected.

"That's very nice of her, but I have some feelers out and expect I'll be able to find something soon."

He nodded and looked insultingly pleased with her refusal. Then he shook his head and frowned, as if reprimanding himself in some way.

"Nonna's business, like all tourist endeavors here, took a hard hit over the last couple of years.

She's still worried that even though things have improved, she won't be able to catch back up financially. Having the extra money from you renting a room would make her feel a bit more secure, so if you don't find anywhere else to go, please consider her offer."

Now, that was understandable, and made it more difficult to refuse. Yet, could she really risk being not only in such constant contact with Massimo, but also immersed in the warm atmosphere of that lovely house? Everything inside shouted that doing so wouldn't be wise, but all she could do was hope she'd find somewhere else while still knowing better than to completely reject the opportunity.

She nodded, saying, "Sure. I'll keep it in mind."

And, by the end of the day, when no one else had come through, she had to acknowledge that Agriturismo Villa Giovanna may be her only option. But if she was going to stay there, she'd be doing it on her own terms, and no one else's.

CHAPTER EIGHT

MASSIMO WAS BOTH relieved and annoyed when he
found out Kendra had asked to be able to leave
the clinic early to run an errand. Since he hadn't
finished examining Mrs. Lionetti the evening
before, he'd arranged with Tino to go back and
complete the elderly lady's checkup, but this time
he had to take Fatima.

"Madonna!" she said, when she saw the still-
impressive pile of rubble. "It's a wonder the injured man survived."

Massimo grunted in agreement, and once more
his brain conjured the image of the rocks shifting,
Kendra not moving out of the way. Sweat broke
out along his brow and spine just remembering it.

Mrs. Lionetti was still so full of excitement
about the building collapse, she omitted her usual
acerbic comments, and the visit was quickly con-
cluded. Massimo had drawn some blood, and
told Tino he wanted her to go to the hospital in
Salerno for additional tests.

"The memory problems you've described are

concerning, and I want to try to discover what's causing them, before they get any worse."

Parting from Fatima not long after, Massimo made his way to his vehicle, which he'd left at the clinic. The streets were full of people, milling about, laughing and talking. A few locals called out to him as he passed, but he simply waved and continued on.

He'd visited the area every summer since he was a boy, even younger than Pietro was now, and had lived here for almost seven years, but there were only a handful of people he'd call friends. He knew he had the reputation of being shy or retiring, but wasn't sure that was accurate. While at medical school in Roma, he'd developed a circle of acquaintances and had an active social life. That time of his life, he'd enjoyed the companionship, even though the living in the city wasn't to his liking. It had seemed appropriate to enjoy the bright lights and sometimes free and easy ways of youth.

That had continued for a while after he moved to Minori. Then, he had been far more outgoing, dining out some evenings, getting together with friends for various activities. It was during that time he'd met Therese, who had been hired as marketing manager at one of the nearby five-star hotels. She'd seemed everything he could wish for—smart, beautiful, charming—and he'd fallen hard from the moment he saw her sultry smile.

That had lasted just under three years. Despite her well-paying job, Therese had wanted to move on. Not out of ambition, but out of boredom with the Amalfi Coast and, he suspected, with him. Their final days together had been fraught with her biting indictments of his character and life, as though ridiculing him would somehow make her case stronger.

Now, when he considered his own shortcomings, instead of his father's jeers, which had haunted his younger self, now it was her voice he heard in his head.

Under those circumstances, was it any wonder that he preferred a quiet life, without fuss or dramatics?

At least that is what he told himself. Although loneliness niggled as he passed a trattoria, crowded with laughing, chatting patrons, and couldn't help looking to see if Kendra was in there.

But his grandmother had been right. His solitary life was a choice, and one he refused to regret. He was too old to change, and too cautious to risk his heart again, so the way things were was for the best.

Driving home, he found himself remembering the night before, when he'd had Kendra to keep him company. Even though much of the conversation was her berating him for going into Mrs. Ricci's house to get her belongings, tonight he found the drive too quiet, even with the radio going.

"Nonna, I'm home," he called out, as he walked in through the door.

"There you are," she said, stepping into the corridor and beaming at him. "I wasn't sure how late you'd be, but now that you're here, we'll eat. Kendra said not to wait for her, and so we won't."

He froze in the act of putting down his medical bag, and stared.

"Kendra?"

"Yes," his grandmother replied, stepping back into the kitchen, her voice fading. "She called to say she might be late, and I told her not to worry. We'll leave the door unlocked for her, and she can just lock it behind her when she comes in."

He was thankful Nonna wasn't looking at him, since he had no idea what the expression on his face was. Composing himself, he went into the kitchen, trying to be nonchalant.

"When did you speak to her?"

"She called this afternoon, about four. Thanked me very much for the offer, and said she would take me up on it. We negotiated a price, and that's when she said she'd be in late."

Massimo stood in the doorway, unsure of whether what he was feeling was annoyance or excitement or both. Whatever it was, he was absolutely sure he didn't like it.

He'd been so sure she wouldn't accept Nonna's invitation, he'd never really considered the impact it would have if she did.

"Did you tell her the bus doesn't run along this route after a certain time?"

Nonna gave a shrug, and tasted the sauce she was stirring, before replying, "I mentioned it, but I am not worried. Your Kendra seems very capable and sensible. I'm sure she already knew that."

But now his mind was already gnawing at the idea of her walking up the steep hill by herself in the dark, although it wasn't really dark yet. Or perhaps accepting a drive from someone who might be unsavory. Or...

"Massimo, stop worrying." Nonna sounded as though she were trying not to laugh. "As our boarder, Kendra can come and go as she pleases, and I will not have you glaring at her as you are now just because she chooses to live her own life."

"I am not glaring," he said, automatically, which made his grandmother chuckle.

"Pietro, is Zio Massimo glaring, or no?"

For the first time in days, he saw Pietro's lips twitch into a little smile. "He is glaring, Nonna Bianchi."

"See? It's a wonder you haven't turned the milk sour with that face."

Massimo forced himself to relax, and smile. "But the milk can't see my face, Nonna, since it is in the refrigerator."

And he was so very happy to hear Pietro laugh.

It worried him, how solemn and silent the little boy was. Not that there was anything wrong with being quiet, as he himself knew all too well. But the feeling that Pietro perhaps wasn't happy here with them gnawed at him all the time. Wanting what was best for a child, and not knowing what that was, was heartbreaking.

"Let me go and wash up for dinner," he said, taking one last fond look at that small smile still on Pietro's face. "And then you both can tell me all about your day."

They had just sat down to eat when Massimo heard the unmistakable sound of a scooter coming up the hill. When it turned into the driveway, he exchanged a startled glance with his grandmother, and excused himself to go to the front door. Occasionally, although infrequently, they had guests turn up looking for accommodation without calling ahead.

But before he could get to the door, it opened and Kendra walked in, knapsack on her back, carrying her duffel and a couple of shopping bags.

She paused when she saw him, and for a long

moment neither of them moved, or spoke. Massimo was aware of his heart thundering, and his muscles tightening, as though preparing for combat, but he tried not to let any of his inner turmoil show.

"I hope you weren't waiting for me to come in," she said, lips in a slight smile that didn't fool him for a moment.

She too looked as though ready for war.

"Of course not," he said, although it had been his intention to do just that. "When I heard the scooter, I didn't know it was you. I thought perhaps it was some tourists looking for lodging."

"Good," she said succinctly, closing and locking the door behind her. Then she started for the staircase. "I don't plan on being a disruption to your family routine, and I certainly don't need babysitting, so it's best to start as we mean to go on."

"Certamente." He was sure she was going to make him crazy over the next months but he'd be damned before he let her know that. "Did you rent the scooter?"

"No. Once I realized it made sense to take your grandmother up on her offer, I went to Salerno and bought it, secondhand. I don't want to have to depend on the bus—or you—to get around."

That shouldn't hurt, but it did.

"Ah, Kendra," his grandmother called from the kitchen. "Did you eat?"

"Yes, I did, thank you, Mrs. Bianchi." She was partway up the stairs, but paused politely.

"Good. Make yourself at home. Later, if you like, I will show you where to find everything."

"Thank you," she said again. "I'd appreciate that."

Then she was gone, and Massimo stood there, staring up after her until he heard her door close with a decisive snap.

Kendra closed her bedroom door, and let out a long breath.

This was such a bad idea, yet she'd had to admit to herself she didn't have a lot of choice when it came to somewhere to stay. None of the other avenues had panned out, and the people she'd spoke to didn't seem terribly optimistic about her chances of finding a new place to rent.

Sighing, she put her bags on the bench near the cupboard and, as though drawn by a magnet, moved to the window to look out at the view. Villa Giovanna was set into the side of the hill, the windows at the back overlooking the terraces below and then out to the distant sea. Beyond a hill she could see a bit of Minori, but the town didn't hold her attention. Instead, she found herself looking down into the gardens and groves below, lushly green and bright with flowers.

There was something about the landscape that called to her, but she refused to answer.

Just like she refused to do more than acknowledge the draw of Massimo Bianchi.

And his family too.

What she really needed to do was set very specific boundaries while she was here.

There would be no coddling. No happy roommates. No becoming part of the family.

To make it work she'd get up early and leave quietly, without stopping for even a cup of coffee—although Mrs. Bianchi had made it clear breakfast and dinner were included in her rent.

Come home late, after they'd already eaten, and go up to her room to watch movies and shows on her tablet.

Take off on the weekends to explore the surrounding area.

Those boundaries were more for her than for the Bianchis.

The atmosphere in the house attracted her deep down, and she knew better than to give in to the lure of "belonging."

That never lasted.

"Belonging" always turned into heartbreak when she once more became an outsider.

She'd long since given up believing she truly could fit in anywhere. Since she was ten, every time she thought she'd found a safe haven and people who wanted her forever, she'd been wrong. And now she was old enough, and wise enough, to know you only got hurt if you allowed others to get too close.

So she kept her distance.

And that's what she needed to do here, especially from Massimo.

He was even more attractive than the atmosphere at Agriturismo Villa Giovanna, especially the longer she worked with him.

A man that big, that solemn, shouldn't be so good with people of every age and condition, and yet he was. On the outside he gave the impression of standoffishness, but she'd seen him charm the crankiest *nonna* or gently calm the most frightened child with ease. With the men he was like a son, or brother, while he treated the younger women with genuine respect.

The first time she heard him sing a silly song to distract a scared baby, something inside her melted, and refused to solidify afterward. Massimo, in all his incarnations, threatened to derail her carefully constructed detachment.

She was honest enough to admit she still wanted him. That she couldn't help remembering just how wonderful he'd made her feel, and acknowledged it was torture to know he was right next door and she couldn't touch him. What she knew, however, was that the only way to survive the situation unscathed was to stay away from him as much as possible. Which was extremely difficult since now they both worked and lived in the same places.

And she needed to stay out of his family life too.

Even now, as she got ready to have her shower, she yearned to go downstairs and join them, be welcomed to take part in their evening ritual.

It was a yearning she'd given in to at every place she'd moved to after her father died, and his family started passing her around from one house to another. At each new relative's home, she'd try to integrate, to find a way to fit in, so she'd be one of the family, but it didn't really work, and soon she'd be passed on again.

Now, all these years later, she better understood that none of them had had the financial ability to raise her alone, and that they'd tried to do the best they could. Yet, the fact that not one of them thought to keep her made her sure there'd been something fundamentally wrong with her. If not, why didn't even one of her aunts or uncles try to find a way for her to stay with them?

No. Keeping a firm, polite distance while at Agriturismo Villa Giovanna was the best thing to do.

Her peace of mind, and her heart, demanded it.

CHAPTER NINE

SHE TRIED HER very best to follow her plan, but it fell apart far quicker than she'd expected.

A week in, to be precise.

That morning, when she opened her door to leave for work, she found a café latte and a pastry on a tray in the passageway. She stared at it for a long moment, considering whether to just ignore it, but she could never be so very rude. Not to someone who'd only ever tried to be nice.

Taking the tray, she went downstairs to thank Mrs. Bianchi, who was bustling about making breakfast for her guests, only to have her shrug in a way Kendra was beginning to realize was habitual.

"Pietro asked if he could take it up for you, and I told him yes. He's a sweet, kind boy and I think he was worried that you were going to work without any breakfast." She smiled, looking out the window to where the little boy sat on a bench, eating an apple, an open book on his lap. "I always tell him he must have something to eat in the morning, since it is oh, so hard to think straight on an empty stomach."

Kendra found herself melting, and tried to pull herself together. It was this kind of nonsense she had to guard against, but how do you harden your heart toward a lovely little boy like that?

"He's always thinking of others." Mrs. Bianchi sighed, still absently drying the plate in her hand, although she must've been in danger of wiping the pattern off. "I think it is because there were so many of them in the orphanage that the older children got used to taking care of the younger."

Oh, Kendra could understand that only too well. Hadn't she always bent over backward to try to help out so as to prove her worth?

It was heartbreaking to see it playing out in another young life.

And now her curiosity was aroused. How had Pietro come to be here? What were Mrs. Bianchi's plans for the youngster, going forward?

Even acknowledging it was none of her business, Kendra couldn't stop herself from asking, "How did you find Pietro?"

Finally putting down the plate, the older lady turned to Kendra. "My daughter-in-law Sophia, Massimo's mother, works for the child welfare agency in Napoli. I was visiting one day, and she asked me if I'd like to go to the orphanage with her, as they were doing a volunteer workday there—cooking a special meal for the children, playing games with them, that sort of thing. Of course, I said yes, and while I was there, I saw Pietro, and knew I had to bring him home with me."

"Just like that?" Kendra asked, unable to mask the skepticism in her voice.

"*Sì*," she replied, with a firm nod. "It was like when I saw my darling husband, all those years ago. Love at first sight. Only this time, it was with a little boy who had no one, and needed to belong somewhere."

Kendra nodded, still unconvinced, but unwilling to say so.

Fingering the cross that hung from a chain around her neck, Mrs. Bianchi continued, "He was left in a *culla per la vita,* a baby hatch, in Napoli when he was just days old. They never found his mother, and he was sent to the orphanage." She placed a gentle hand on Kendra's arm, and said, "Sometimes, you just know something is right, and meant to be, and I knew that as soon as I saw him. I am too old to adopt him, but Massimo and I have decided that Pietro will always have a home here, with us, no matter what may happen."

Swallowing hard, Kendra didn't reply, ridiculously touched and unwilling to show it. Finally, when she was sure her voice would sound normal, she smiled and said, "Let me go and thank Pietro for my breakfast."

Then, taking her coffee with her, she slipped out through the glass doors into the cool of the morning, stopping to take a few steadying breaths before walking over to sit beside Pietro. He looked up, his too-old blue eyes surveying her for a moment before returning to his book.

"Good morning. I wanted to thank you for the coffee and pastry," she said. "It was very nice of you to bring them up for me."

"You're welcome," he said, his gaze steadfast on the page in front of him.

"What are you reading?"

Keeping his place with one finger, he flipped the book closed to show her the cover. "It's about two boys who run away to have an adventure."

"Is it any good?" she asked, amused at his succinct description.

He shrugged, the gesture so much like Mrs. Bianchi's signature shoulder movement it made Kendra smile.

"It's not bad, but I think they are really quite silly. When they left home, they took nothing useful or handy, just some bread and water."

"Well, at least they have some food. And everyone needs water to survive, don't they?"

Earnest blue eyes looked back up at her, as Pietro nodded. "*Sì*. But why do they have no compass, or even a map? And look at their shoes." He pointed to the cover, his finger touching the sneakers the boys were wearing. Old-school sneakers, with canvas tops and rubber toes, like the ones basketball players used to wear. "They are supposed to be going through rough terrain. Their feet should be hurting, all the time, and yet they never are."

So much logic from such a little chap. It made Kendra want to laugh, but she squelched the urge, knowing he would probably misunderstand. Instead, she nodded in agreement.

"You're right. They were being silly or, at the very least, not thinking things through properly before they started."

"Exactly." He nodded approvingly, his lips twitching up just slightly at the corners. "They didn't plan at all well, but I'll keep reading to see how it all turns out."

"I understand," she replied, keeping her face solemn. "I don't like not finishing a book I start either."

They exchanged a glance of sheer and complete understanding, and once more Kendra's heart melted. He really was the sweetest little fellow.

But there was still the matter she came out here to discuss with him. "While I appreciate the coffee this morning, Pietro, you don't need to bring me breakfast every day."

The smile faded and his eyes grew shuttered as he nodded silently, and she felt the connection they'd developed start to disintegrate.

"Why don't I come down and have breakfast before I leave, instead?"

His gaze flew back to her face, and he looked at her carefully, as if judging and weighing her words. Then he seemed to relax, and he nodded.

"That would be good. Nonna Bianchi wouldn't worry so much, then." She tried not to react to his words, but must have shown something, because he rushed on. "She worries about everyone. Zio Massimo, her family in Napoli, the guests who visit, even me."

Oh, Lord, this little man was dead set on breaking her heart completely, wasn't he? And what on earth was she supposed to say to that, when she completely understood exactly how he felt? Once you became used to being an afterthought, or a burden others had to bear, it was so difficult to break free from those thoughts.

But his situation was very different from the one she went through, and she wished there was some way to be reassuring, without making him feel she was just spouting platitudes.

"Pietro…" Her voice broke slightly, and she had to stop, swallow, clear her throat before she could continue. "Pietro, everyone deserves to be worried over. Besides, Nonna Bianchi doesn't just worry for no reason. She worries because she cares. Because she loves. And love isn't like a cake, that once you've cut it and eaten it, it's gone. Love lasts forever, no matter what."

Once more that probing blue gaze turned her way, and his eyebrows rose slightly.

"But how can she love so much?"

She said the first thing that came to mind. "I think we all can, if we allow ourselves to, and if we get enough practice, and Nonna Bianchi has had a lot of time to get it right."

He considered that for a long moment, and she could almost see those logical gears in his mind turning over. Then he nodded.

"*Sì*, she is very old, and must have had a lot of people to practice on."

Kendra couldn't help the little chuckle that broke from her throat. "That's true, but maybe you shouldn't mention her age to her. Ladies don't like being called ancient."

To her surprise, Pietro giggled, and she couldn't help laughing with him, mostly from relief from having navigated a sticky conversation without getting all tangled up.

"Come on," she said, getting to her feet. "I need to get to work."

"Okay." Pietro carefully marked his place in

his book, and got up too. As they walked back toward the house, he said, "I thought of something else those boys should have taken with them, on their adventure. A pocketknife."

"That's a good one," she said, as he opened the kitchen door for her, and stood back a little for her to precede him into the room. What a gentleman. "How about matches? In case they need to light a fire, and cook?"

"Ah! *Sì!* That is also a good one." He was beaming, as though she were the smartest person he'd ever met. "What else?"

She stepped through the door, and there was Massimo, sitting at the table, watching them. There was no way to gauge what his expression meant, but it sent alternating waves of hot and cold through her body.

"Cheese," she said, not knowing where that came from, but when Pietro laughed, she added, "I love cheese, and would *never* go on an adventure without some."

Which, thankfully, made Pietro laugh even harder, and allowed her to break free from focusing on Zio Massimo's face.

There'd been enough of having her heartstrings tugged on for the day, thank you very much.

The clinic was busy with waves of tourist patients, but although Massimo was kept hopping all morning, whenever he had a free moment his mind immediately turned to Kendra.

And Pietro.

How had she so easily broken through the little boy's normal reticence and got him to laugh like that?

Not that Pietro never smiled or laughed, but usually it took a great deal of effort to make it happen. Effort Massimo tried to put in, but that was not always successful either.

And the smile on her face had a different tone to it as well. As though all of her usual smiles and laughter were a facade, and this moment of enjoyment—of connection—was the real one.

Did that include the smiles and laughter she'd shared with him in bed?

He tried to think back to that night, which seemed horribly long ago, but the memory was clouded by a fog of lust and passion, and couldn't be trusted.

"Dr. Bianchi? We have a Japanese tourist being brought in following a fall at Villa Romana. The ambulance personnel report that he was traveling alone, and speaks no Italian and little English."

Before he could respond, he heard that familiar voice from behind him say, "I speak some Japanese. Perhaps I can translate."

Of course she would be the one to assist, at the

time when he really least wanted to be around her, but Massimo bit back a sigh and nodded.

"Thank you."

He tried not to sound as grudgeful as he felt, but knew he hadn't been successful when she chuckled, which just brought on that crazy spike of need that drove through him any time he heard her do so.

She was driving him quietly insane. Just knowing she was in the house at night kept him awake and awash with desire. He was becoming so irritable, Nonna was avoiding speaking to him as much as possible. Strangely, though, his grandmother hadn't asked him what was wrong. Normally she'd have been probing at him like a dentist at a sore tooth, trying to find the root of the problem.

It was going to be an excruciating few months until she left.

But the thought of her leaving, and things going back to normal, just made him more edgy.

The Japanese patient was brought in with a laceration on his arm and a bump on the back of his head. According the Kendra, he was apologizing and saying he didn't need to be in the hospital, and although he couldn't understand what she was saying in reply, Massimo had no doubt she was being reassuring.

That was something he'd noticed about her—

that there was a deep well of understanding and empathy beneath her jocularity and seemingly easygoing nature. Patients and coworkers alike gravitated to her and seemed to feel completely comfortable in her presence.

"He says he was walking backward, looking up, and didn't pay attention to where he was going. He thinks he slipped on a stone, and he put out his hand to try to grab onto anything to stop from falling, but cut his arm instead as he fell."

"Hematoma above the lower left parietal bone, but no signs of concussion. Ask if he's feeling nauseous or sleepy."

As Kendra asked the patient what he wanted to know, Massimo examined the laceration on Mr. Tanaka's arm.

"He admits to a headache, but none of the other symptoms. How is his arm?"

"Not too severe a cut, but it will need stitches. How long will he be in the area? He'll have to get the stitches removed in about ten days."

After some conversation, she said, "He'll be back home by then, and he promises he'll go to his doctor in Nagasaki and get them removed."

"Good." Massimo gave the other man a smile, but found Mr. Tanaka's gaze was trained on Kendra's face, and his expression made Massimo clench his teeth. "I'll clean and suture his arm…"

"Oh?" Kendra raised an eyebrow. "I can do that. You have other patients waiting."

"I like to take care of these things myself, for the tourists, when I can." True but, in this case, he had a definite ulterior motive—removing Kendra from the equation. "And that will free you up to take vitals on the next patient."

"But you won't be able to speak to Mr. Tanaka if you need to."

"I think we've covered everything necessary. If you tell him what's going to happen, you can give him the instructions about his wound before he leaves."

He thought he sounded reasonable, but Kendra gave him a long look and he thought she was going to laugh, but she held it back.

"Sure," she said, the corners of her lips twitching.

She spoke to Mr. Tanaka, and the disappointment on the other man's face was obvious. When his patient finally looked at Massimo, he knew his smile wasn't as kind as it could be.

But he didn't care.

CHAPTER TEN

THE PROBLEM WITH making concessions is that once you started, it was difficult not to keep giving ground. Which is how Kendra came to be having dinner with the Bianchi family one Thursday night, about two weeks after she'd first moved in.

It was impossible to say no to Pietro when he invited her, especially when he added, "It would make Nonna Bianchi happy, I think."

"Will it make you happy?" she asked, wanting him to know that, to her, his happiness was just as important.

And when he nodded, a tiny, hopeful smile tipping the edges of his mouth, she had to agree, even knowing being around Massimo was becoming achingly difficult.

While there was no escaping her physical reactions to him, it was his other attributes that had captured and held her attention.

The gentleness. His ability to make anyone he was speaking to feel as though he was completely focused on them. The way he treated his grand-mother and Pietro.

Then there was the sight of him, one morning, just as the sun was rising, down among the lemon trees, carefully tending the plants and picking fruit for his grandmother.

Something about his demeanor, his calm surety as he moved from plant to plant, the motion of his hands—almost caressing—made her heart race, and a warm space open in her chest.

The more she got to know him, the more beautiful she found him, and she knew, deep inside, he presented a fundamental danger to her.

Exactly what that danger was, she wasn't sure. But it existed, and she didn't know how to handle it, or what to do.

And if she wasn't already aware of how strong the attraction was growing, it became completely clear on her last sightseeing trip, the weekend before. Although she'd made a point of coming down and having coffee in the kitchen before going to work each morning, she'd also made sure to make herself scarce most of the rest of the time. The first weekend after moving into Villa Giovanna, she'd taken a friend's suggestion and gone to explore Vietri sul Mare and the neighboring Cetara.

Neither of those small villages got the massive influx of tourists some of the other Amalfi

Coast towns did, and the quiet, more laid-back atmosphere should have been calming. Yet, while she'd tried to enjoy the beauty surrounding her, investigating the myriad pottery stores in Vietri and enjoying the wonderful cuisine, the entire trip had felt surprisingly flat. It was as though something vital had been missing.

Again and again she'd found her mind turning to Massimo, wondering what he was doing, until she'd gotten completely annoyed with herself. She'd been tempted to cut her visit short, but forced herself to stay until Sunday, as planned.

So, when Pietro had invited her to join them for dinner, she'd really wanted to refuse. Nevertheless, having given her word, she presented herself at the dinner table, a little self-consciously but with her chin up, unwilling to let any of them see how unsure she was.

Mrs. Bianchi and Pietro greeted her with broad smiles, while Massimo gave her a comprehensive once-over that made her glad she'd changed into a knit sundress for the occasion. She'd also let her hair down, catching it back with a brightly colored band and letting it wave down her back.

"How lovely you look," Mrs. Bianchi said. "I don't know how you manage to be so chic while living out of a suitcase all the time."

It shouldn't be gratifying, but Kendra couldn't

help the little glow of pride the older lady's words gave her.

"I long ago discovered the joys of knit clothing," she replied, with a grin. "And I tend to follow the sun, so I don't need heavy winter clothes. That makes packing light a lot easier too."

"I think your ingenuity and adventurous spirit is wonderful. I'm afraid I couldn't do what you do." Mrs. Bianchi looked around the cheerful kitchen, and shook her head. "I went from my parents' home to my husband's, and just…never left."

While her tone was rueful, there was no hint of sadness, and Kendra found herself wanting to say that she didn't blame her in the slightest. That life at Villa Giovanna seemed idyllic, so it was completely understandable. But, just then, Kendra's gaze got tangled up with Massimo's and, as her heart went into overdrive, she bit back the words.

The seemed too intimate, suddenly.

Too revealing.

But she realized halfway through the meal that all her reticence and hesitations had disappeared, as the conversation ebbed and flowed from topic to topic, drawing her in. The dynamic within the family was easy to become a part of, keeping her engaged and making her comfortable.

"Where are you off to this weekend?" Mrs. Bianchi asked, as Kendra helped her clear the table, and Massimo went to the fridge for the limoncello.

"Someone suggested I go to Capri, but the week has been so busy, I haven't made any real plans. I do have tomorrow off as well, though, so I might just do a day trip. I doubt Fridays are as busy as the weekend would be there."

"Oh, Capri is beautiful." Mrs. Bianchi gave a decisive nod. "You really should go. Massimo, do you know if Sergio is going to be at his villa this weekend?"

Who on earth was Sergio?

"I think he's still in Venice, on that project," Massimo said. "He's not due back for another couple of weeks."

"Well, then, you should call him and ask if you can stay at his villa and take Kendra to Capri. I know you're off tomorrow too, so you could make a long weekend of it."

"Oh, that's not—"

"I don't think—"

Both she and Massimo spoke at the same time, and stopped at the same time, which made Mrs. Bianchi look from one of them to the other. Yet, after that, she changed the subject, as though nothing untoward at all had happened.

Risking a glance at Massimo, she found him looking at her from under his lashes, and there was no mistaking his expression.

Desire.

Heat encompassed her entire body and Kendra tore her gaze away, but she knew without a doubt, should they go to Capri—or anywhere else— together, what would happen.

The lust swirling between them was unmistakable, and undeniable, no matter how hard she tried to ignore it or will it away.

Thankfully, just then, Pietro suddenly said, "Zio Massimo, why do you have a car, while Signorina Kendra has a scooter?"

Massimo's eyebrows rose, but he replied in his usual calm way, "I drive a car because I sometimes need to go longer distances, like when I visit Napoli. Besides, I have to carry my medical bag with me wherever I go."

Pietro seemed to consider that answer for a moment, and then said, "But Signorina Kendra carried all her clothes and everything here on her scooter, so there must be room. And I think her scooter is much nicer than your car. Wouldn't you prefer to ride a scooter?"

Relieved at the change of subject, and thoroughly tickled, Kendra bit her lip to hold back her laughter at the thought of Massimo giving up his comfortable luxury car for a small motorbike. But it became harder to contain her mirth when she glanced at Massimo's expression. He was trying so hard to remain serious in the face of the little boy's questions, but there was a decidedly amused twinkle in his eyes.

"I used to ride a scooter when I was young, at university in Roma, and it was a great deal of fun then."

Once more the little boy gave his reply some thought, then asked, "Was that so very long ago that you wouldn't like it anymore?"

Kendra choked on the chuckle that rose into her throat. Was the little devil calling Massimo old, without actually saying it?

For his part, Massimo stared blandly at Pietro for a long beat, and then said, "After I've finished my *digestivo*, with Signorina Kendra's permission, I'll show you that I am indeed still quite capable of riding a scooter."

She couldn't hold back her laughter anymore, even when Massimo sent her a glance best described as smoldering—which sent a thrill of need through her body.

"Oh," she gasped, hoping everyone blamed her breathlessness on her amusement, rather than deep desire. "Of course you may. I look forward to seeing that."

"You will most certainly see it," he replied, giving her a look from beneath his long lashes. "For you will be on the back of the scooter with me."

"Will I, now?" She tried to keep her voice

amused and level, but her heart was suddenly pounding, and she knew she'd failed.

"Indeed," he replied, his voice deep and slow, which ridiculously increased the heat rushing through her veins. "I insist on it."

Mrs. Bianchi clicked her tongue and said, "When I was young, a boy asking me to ride on the back of his scooter was something my parents wouldn't approve of. In fact, the only person whose scooter I rode on, I ended up marrying."

"Luckily for us all, times have changed, Nonna."

It shouldn't annoy her to hear him say that. After all, she agreed with him. Yet, she had to squash a spurt of irritation.

"Not always for the better," the elderly lady answered. "Not always for the better."

"Perhaps you're right, Nonna." Massimo was looking down at his limoncello, those thick fingers twisting the glass back and forth, his eyes hidden so she couldn't read their expression. "There are definitely times when some of those silent but easily understood signals would be useful to have."

Was it her imagination, or was there a deeper meaning to his words? And was that cryptic message meant for her?

Just then his lashes rose, and he met her gaze with one that momentarily flashed with unmistakable fire. Heat that transferred itself right into her body and ricocheted—like a lightning strike—through her blood.

Which of them looked away first, she didn't know, but if she'd held his gaze a moment more, it would be impossible not to reveal the desire heightening her senses and making her thighs tremble.

She laughed—more to relieve the nervous energy sparking beneath her skin than anything else—and from the corner of her eye she saw Massimo tip the last of his *digestivo* into his mouth.

"Come, then," he said, getting to his feet. "Let us take a ride, Signorina Kendra."

And, for her, there really was no mistaking his meaning now.

"With pleasure," she replied, without thinking it through, which made her chuckle again.

Perhaps Kendra thought they'd just go to the end of the driveway and back to the house, but Massimo had other plans. It was time to get the situation between them straight, before he did something embarrassing, like try to kiss the amusement off her lips.

Under Pietro's watchful eyes, and Nonna's somewhat worried gaze, he got the scooter off the stand, and straddled it. After he'd started it,

he looked back at Kendra, who was still chuck-
ling, the sound going straight through his soul
and sending his libido into overdrive.

She needed no prompting, but came and got
onto the seat behind him and, snuggling herself
to his back, put her arms around his waist. For
them both to fit, he had to sit far forward, with
his long legs bent slightly out, and he knew she
couldn't be terribly comfortable, but she didn't
complain.

And he realized, now, why his grandmother
hadn't been allowed to ride on the back of men's
scooters when she was young. There was something incredibly sensual about knowing he was
cradled between Kendra's bare, spread thighs,
and the way her arms gripped his waist. Not to
mention the sensation of her lush breasts pressing against his back.

As he opened the throttle, the thought came to
him that if she moved her hand down, just a little,
she'd be able to grasp his erection. His instinctive
reaction to that image made the scooter wobble.

Which made Kendra laugh even harder.

Which made him even harder.

In the distance he heard Pietro shout something, but couldn't make out the words. Then they
were out the gate, and he was steering the vehicle
up the hill, away from Minori. The family land
extended for several acres on both sides of the

road, and he had a special place in mind to take Kendra. It was one of his favorite spots on the property, and one few people knew even existed, and so would be deserted.

The road switched back, and he took the tight corner as fast as he dared. He was rewarded for his bravado when Kendra let out a *whoop* of enjoyment. Here, now, the land leveled off a little, and what looked like an untamed woodland lay to their right. He slowed and, once he was sure no traffic was coming, swerved onto the track into the trees. Slowing even more, they bumped along for a few yards, then he brought the scooter to a halt, and turned it off.

Putting his feet down to steady the bike, he waited for Kendra to alight, but she stayed where she was, arms tight around him, those delicious breasts firm against his back.

"What is this place?" she asked, her breath warm against his neck.

"It is part of the upper acreage of the farm," he replied, doing his best to keep his voice even, although his heart was pounding. "While it's cultivated farther along, we keep this part mostly wild, except for one place, which I'd like to show you."

Was it his imagination, or did her arms tighten slightly, before she let go and got off the scooter?

"Lead on," she said, as he put the scooter on the stand.

Getting off, he held out his hand, his breath catching in his chest until she took it, twining her fingers through his. The stand of trees wasn't very big, and he knew this land better than almost anyone alive, so it took only a minute or so to guide her to the spot.

"Oh!" The wonder in her voice, as she stared out at the field of wildflowers, made his heart sing. "Massimo, how beautiful. How did this come to be here?"

"My grandfather made this clearing in the trees and sowed seeds of native flowering plants to make sure his neighbor's bees would never lack for nectar and pollen. It's beautiful in spring, but this is the perfect time to see it, although different plants bloom all the way through to autumn."

She was still holding his hand, and her fingers tightened around his, but she didn't say anything.

Although he'd always loved this place, her stunned, silent appreciation caused him to look at the field in a new way. As though seeing it for the first time, instead of the thousandth.

The scent of the flowers rose in the warm air, and the low buzz of the last bees of the evening could be heard on the breeze. But it was the waves of colored petals that gave the field its beauty and majesty. Sometimes it was easy to take such sights for granted, or to focus on the ephemeral nature of the blooms, rather than living in the now. With intention, and the knowledge that life was too short not to grasp opportunities with both hands when they were presented.

"I want you." He said it as he felt it, with conviction, and no restraint. "And I wanted you to know it."

Once more she squeezed his fingers, but then she withdrew her hand from his. Still staring out at the flowers, she took an audible breath, and he couldn't help noticing that she didn't laugh.

He filed that away for later consideration.

"I want you too," she finally said, in a tone that conveyed nothing but the factual nature of her feelings. "But I respect your grandmother far too much to conduct any kind of ongoing affair under her roof."

"Understandable." And, in his mind, commendable.

"And," she continued, before he could say anything more, "you need to know there can be no emotional involvement. I'll be gone in a matter of months, and I don't like drama."

"Also understandable, and I don't like dramatics either."

As for a lack of emotional involvement, he would try his hardest not to get in any way attached. In this they were also in accord.

She'd been looking out over the field as she spoke, but now turned to search his face with an intent gaze.

"There also can't be any kind of weirdness at work. If we can't maintain our professional relationship at the clinic, then it would be best we don't get further involved."

He shrugged. "We slept together before you came to the clinic, and I think you'd agree we've been able to work together completely harmoniously, and without difficulties."

Kendra's eyebrows rose, as though she was about to argue the point, but then she just shook her head and said, "If you can figure out a way for us to be together that doesn't include your grandmother being aware of it, I'd be interested."

Her tone would suggest she were talking about a job, or some other mundane matter, rather than the heart-stopping opportunity he felt it to be. And he was tempted to match her sangfroid, but something within rebelled against pretending a disinterest he truly didn't feel.

So, instead of replying, he stepped close, and pulled her into his arms.

"Let's make sure this is something we want to pursue," he said, dipping his lips close to hers, gratified to realize her breathing was rushed, relieved when she didn't hesitate to wrap her arms around his neck.

When she pulled his head down the final inch so their lips met, and immediately deepened the kiss into the realm of carnal and arousing, Massimo thought the top of his head would explode.

Finally, knowing that if they didn't stop, he would ease her down into the flowers and take the encounter to the next level, he reluctantly drew away. But they stayed locked together for another few long beats, as he drowned in the depth of her aroused, heavy-lidded gaze.

"Was there ever a doubt we'd want to pursue it?" she asked, the question obviously a rhetorical one.

Then, when she followed it up with a delicious round of laughter, it took all of his control to let her go.

CHAPTER ELEVEN

HE SUGGESTED THEY take advantage of his grandmother's suggestion and go to Capri the following day.

"My cousin Sergio is an actor and owns a villa on the island," he said, as he casually withdrew a small knife from his pocket. Opening it, he began to pick a handful of flowers. "If he's in agreement, we can stay there. If it isn't available, I can find us another place."

With an electric current still humming through her veins from their kisses, Kendra eagerly agreed. It had taken all of her willpower to let him go, instead of dragging him down into the flowers and having her way with him.

Bees, bugs and potential thorns be damned.

"Oh," she said, surprised and dangerously touched when he presented her with the flowers. "I'll try not to crush them on the ride down."

His lips quirked into a sly smile, as they made their way back to where the motorbike was parked. "And I'll try to be a bit more sedate with how I operate the scooter. There was something about having you behind me that made me rash."

As it turned out, they didn't have to do anything in furtherance of their planned excursion, having an unwitting coconspirator in their proposed affair. By the time they got back to Villa Giovanna, Massimo's grandmother had already contacted Sergio and arranged their accommodation.

"He said you should text him if you need the housekeeper to be on duty while you're there. Otherwise, he'll arrange for her to meet you in the morning and hand over the keys."

"I think we can manage on our own for such a short time," Massimo replied in a bland tone that sent little shivers over Kendra's skin, raising goose bumps in their wake.

She definitely wanted to have him alone in that villa, to do all manner of naughty things with and to him. Having someone else in the house didn't fit in with her plans at all.

Now that she'd made the decision to sleep with him again, she was all in. She'd never been a halfway type of person, and this situation called for a full-on assault. After all, hadn't she spent the last weeks desperately keeping her lust for him in check? Having given and received the green light to get back into bed together, she wanted everything she could get from him, and she had to lock her trembling knees as she considered what the next day might bring.

Thankfully, just then Pietro came barreling through the door into the kitchen.

"Zio, *signorina*, you are back. You were gone so long, I thought you had gone on an adventure far away."

Kendra couldn't help the little bubble of mirth that flew from her lips. "Zio Massimo took me to the flower field up the hill." Showing him the flowers she still had in her hand, she continued. "It is too late in the evening for adventures, especially if they involve pirates. I'm not fond of pirates."

"Zio Massimo would protect you." Pietro mimed pulling a sword and danced about, as though in the midst of an intense fight. "No pirate could harm you if he's there."

His fancy footwork had him bouncing into Mrs. Bianchi, who put out a hand to steady herself against the counter and said, "Careful there, Pietro."

Although she didn't sound cross at all, the little boy froze, his eyes widening in apparent fear, and Kendra felt her heart contract in sympathy. Before she could say anything, though, Massimo intervened.

"I think a proper sword fight should be conducted outside, don't you?" When Pietro didn't move, Massimo crossed the kitchen toward him, saying, "Come, young squire. Let us take up arms and practice to defeat our common foe."

Mrs. Bianchi ran a gentle hand over the little boy's hair, and said softly, "It is all right, Pietro. Go with Zio Massimo and play in the garden."

Obediently Pietro took Massimo's outstretched hand, and they went out together. As they walked away, Kendra could see the stiffness in both their gaits and hear the rise and fall of Massimo's deep voice, but not the words. Drawn to the pair, she moved closer to the door, and found herself standing beside Mrs. Bianchi, who'd done the same.

As man and boy moved across the grass toward the small shed at the edge of the garden, the older woman sighed.

"I worry about Pietro. Sometimes I think he's settled in completely, and is happy, and then…"

Kendra understood, and patted the other woman's shoulder.

"It will take time for him to fully feel secure."

She was speaking from experience.

It was only too easy to remember the feeling of waiting, wondering when, exactly, she'd be rejected again, and have to leave wherever she was. The sensation of walking on eggshells, afraid that if she did anything wrong, no matter how small, she'd be punished and sent away. Never wanting to make a mistake. Always trying her hardest to be good.

Perfect.

And yet, knowing that eventually she'd be shuffled off, proving once more that she was somehow unlovable, and easy to get rid of.

She didn't say any of that, though, and as Mrs. Bianchi had grown silent too, she simply watched Massimo march back out of the shed, Pietro like a little shadow behind him.

"Oh, dear," Nonna said, amusement now tingeing her voice. "The canes I use to tie up my plants are now to be swords. I wonder if they'll survive."

Kendra chuckled, tickled, and moved to see Massimo earnestly instructing Pietro on the classic dueling stance, and best way to hold the "sword."

"It's doubtful," she replied, as Pietro launched a somewhat timid attack on Massimo. "I hope you have more on hand."

"I do," she replied, giving the scene outside one more look before turning away. "Let me get you a vase for your flowers."

Kendra stayed put, her gaze fixed on the pair outside, watching as, little by little, they both relaxed, their earnest expressions morphing slowly into frank enjoyment as they play-fought.

So engrossed was she that she didn't even hear Mrs. Bianchi come back and stand beside her again.

"Isn't it strange how difficult it is to build confidence in oneself?" the older lady asked, in a musing tone. "Some people seem to do it effortlessly, while others need constant reassurance to develop it."

Kendra nodded in agreement. "And there are times I wish I could wave a magic wand and give it away to those who need and deserve it most."

A warm hand touched her arm, giving it a squeeze. "I do too, and have for a long time." The last part seemed incongruous to their conversation, but before Kendra could reply, Mrs. Bianchi added, "Here. Give me your flowers, and go out to join them. I'm sure you could teach them a thing or two."

Wanting to go was instinctual, but so was her hesitation. Mrs. Bianchi took the flowers from her unresisting fingers and gave her a little push between the shoulder blades.

"Go."

So she went, and her heart did a silly flip when both Massimo and Pietro saw her and grinned in welcome.

Massimo did his best to get Pietro involved in their game, and thought he was doing a fairly good job, until Kendra came out to join in and he saw the little boy light up.

Not that he minded. It was truly heartwarming to see Pietro come to life in that way, but it did make him wonder why Kendra was so easily able to connect with the child, while Massimo had to work so hard at it.

After Nonna called Pietro in to take his bath, and dusk was setting in, Massimo stopped Kendra from going into the house with a touch on her arm.

"Thank you for being so good to Pietro. He lets go and is just a child with you, while sometimes..."

He couldn't find the words to express what he was trying to say, but even in the gloom he saw the understanding in Kendra's eyes.

"It's probably because he knows I'm just a visitor, and have no bearing on whether he stays here or not."

Her words drove through him, freezing his blood for a moment.

"We treat him like family. Why would he think we were going to send him away?"

She hesitated, then gestured for him to follow her to the nearby bench. Once they sat down, she turned so she could look at him, and said, "Pietro has never *had* a family. How would he know what it feels like to be treated as a part of one?"

He could find no good answer, and while he sought one, Kendra sighed and rubbed at her cheek.

"It's not the same, but because of my own up-bringing, I can understand why he acts the way he does."

There was no mistaking the reluctance in her voice, as though she'd have preferred not to talk about it, but felt compelled to do so anyway. No doubt for Pietro's sake.

And although there was no emotion in her voice when she next spoke, he realized that was just a smokescreen to hide her real pain.

"I was raised by my father, who'd been at university when I was born. And since he wasn't able to continue his studies with a newborn to look after, he went back to his mother's house in Nova Scotia. Then, like his father before him, he went back to fishing to earn a living."

She paused, turning her face to gaze into the evening gloom, instead of at him, and Massimo found himself holding his breath.

"He died in an accident when I was ten."

Again, a total lack of emotion, but the enormity of what she was saying vibrated in the air between them.

"I'm sorry," he said softly, receiving a chopping motion of her hand in response.

"It was a long time ago, and not the point I'm trying to make. After Dad died, my grandmother did her best to take care of me, but she couldn't manage on her own. All of my father's siblings lived in Ontario—a different province—and decided they'd each take turns looking after me. So, they passed me from place to place until I was old enough to take care of myself.

"All I wanted was the security of a family, like I'd had with Daddy and Grammy, and each time I had to move on, I'd get more withdrawn—more fearful. I'd be on tenterhooks, worried that if I caused even the slightest trouble, I'd have to leave."

She took a deep breath, and faced him once more.

"What I'm trying to tell you is that until Pietro *knows* he is a part of a family—not is *treated* as though he is—there will always be the fear in the back of his mind he'll be rejected. Even if he was adopted there may be times he'll still be unsure, trying not to do anything to make that happen. It will take a long time for him to believe it's forever, and not instinctively assume he's disposable."

He knew she was only telling him these things to try to help him understand what Pietro was going through, but Massimo had so many questions he wanted to ask. About what happened between her parents, her experiences after her father died, and if those experiences were the reason she lived the way she did. Never settling anywhere. Always on the move.

Yet, he knew she wouldn't appreciate his prying, so he said, "What do you suggest I do, then? Nonna has been deemed too old to formally adopt him."

"Why don't you do it, then?"

He should have seen that coming, but her question struck him hard in the chest, and he found himself shaking his head instinctively.

"I can't. The law won't allow it, since I'm unmarried."

Her gaze was searching, and he wondered if she somehow could see through his words to the heart of the matter.

Even if he could, he doubted he would be the type of father Pietro needed, and was unwilling to risk the little boy's happiness and future by being unable to parent him properly. Just as Pietro didn't know what it felt like to be a part of a family, Massimo didn't know what being an involved, encouraging father looked like either, and he lacked the confidence to try.

Kendra's eyes narrowed, and the corners of her lips turned down.

"That's a rather archaic law, I think, and a shame in this situation. So, what exactly do you plan to do? Suppose something happens to your *nonna*? Will they come and take him away?"

"My mother assures me she will help me retain foster parent status if Nonna is unable to take care of him."

"But what if your mother is no longer in a position to do so?" Her tone had gone from curious to concerned. "Massimo, you should find out if there is some way to be appointed co-fosterer with your grandmother, just to make sure."

His heart was now pounding, and a trickle of sweat crawled down his spine.

"Kendra…" He sought the right words, fumbling under the intensity of her scrutiny. "I don't know how to be a father figure to him—how to make sure I'm giving him all he needs."

Her gaze was intent, as though she sought the source of his misgivings. And when, without warning, she grasped his wrist, her fingers were surprisingly cold against his skin.

"No one does, really, when they become a first-time parent. Whatever your hesitations, get over them, for Pietro's sake. You care about him. I can see it, and I know it's not just that he lives here, or that your *nonna* loves him. You have the wherewithal to give him what he needs—a stable, forever home. Don't deny him—and yourself—the opportunity to have a happy life together, because you won't make the right decision."

Then she let him go, and stood up to look down at him, her eyes darker than usual, all of her habitual laughter notably gone from both expression and voice.

"It's scary for you, but think how much scarier it is for Pietro. Being shown this lovely life, with people he's growing to love and depend on, but knowing it can all be taken away in a moment." She shook her head, a wry twist to her lips. "Believe me, I'm not judging you or trying to tell you what to do, but I'm asking you to just think about what I've said, okay?"

How he wished he could be honest with her—tell her that while he wanted, with all his heart, to see Pietro grow up in a loving, protective family, he didn't know how to go about making that happen.

Sometimes he thought that, through example, his own father had shown him what not to do, but then he remembered how his brothers had seemingly thrived under their papa's parenting style. Was the fact that he and his father had such a strained relationship not so much a deficiency in Papa, but one in Massimo instead?

Trying to work it all out and determine how to do the right thing for Pietro left Massimo in a mental and emotional tangle he didn't know how to sort through.

Besides, since his prospects of marrying were nonexistent, there was no chance of adopting

Pietro either, or giving him the nuclear family, including a mother, he deserved.

Yet, there was no way to say any of this, and while it was tempting to dismiss her words out of hand, he also knew she was only trying to help.

And hearing her story made his heart ache for her, but she wouldn't appreciate his sympathy, or curiosity.

So, instead, he said, "I will give it serious thought, and speak to my mama too, to hear what she suggests."

Kendra's smile lit up her entire face, and his heart once more raced, but for a far more carnal reason.

"Good," she said, and then reached out to twine a curl of his hair around her finger, just for a moment, the movement catching him by surprise. "I'm glad."

Then she walked toward the house, leaving him on the bench with his muddled thoughts.

CHAPTER TWELVE

KENDRA WAS REMINDED once more of the fact that when Massimo had come to a decision, there was no hesitancy in putting a plan into motion. Before the end of Thursday evening he had the trip arranged, and suggested they awaken early and take the bus to Sorrento to catch one of the first ferries across the Gulf of Naples.

"During the high season, nonresident cars aren't allowed on the island," he'd explained. "So it doesn't make sense to drive. I hope that'll be okay with you?"

Kendra was used to not only traveling light but also roughing it, so she'd laughed and said, "Sounds positively luxurious in comparison to some of the trips I've been on."

"I'd like to hear more about your travels." He said it casually, but there was an undertone in his voice she didn't understand. "I've hardly been anywhere outside of Europe."

"The kind of life I live isn't for everyone," she

replied, trying to figure out where the conversation was going. "Most people need roots to feel grounded."

Massimo's gaze was searching, and he seemed set to say something more on the subject, but didn't.

Then, the next morning, as they walked down the driveway to get the bus, he said, "I hope I don't have to say this, but I will anyway, so there can be no misunderstanding between us. As desperately as I want to get you back into my bed, I truly do plan to show you the best of Capri. I don't want you to think…"

She held up her hand to stop him.

"I won't lie and say the thought of us spending the weekend in bed didn't cross my mind, but while I think I'd like that very much, I've also learned you're a man of your word. So, since you said you'd show me the sights, I figured you'd do just that."

That gained her one of his sideways glances, but no answer. Sometimes his reticence, which seemed habitual, was both mysterious and frustrating.

She'd been rather hoping he'd change his mind about their itinerary once she said she was okay with not seeing even one of Capri's many sites. The way she was feeling, she'd be quite happy to see only the inside of his cousin's villa, as long as it meant she'd get some relief from the constant thrum of desire she felt around Massimo.

Even so, she also had to acknowledge how dangerous it was to give in to her longing for him. If she'd had any doubts about that, they had been laid to rest the night before, as they spoke about Pietro, and she'd opened up to him about her past.

She'd seen his curiosity, and the genuine sympathy in his eyes, and had been glad he'd refrained from asking any questions.

One of the few times his reserve worked in her favor.

It had been far too easy to tell him the parts she'd confided, considering she never, ever spoke about what had happened after her father died. And it had been oh so tempting to tell him the rest. To finally have someone outside of Koko she could talk to about everything.

Someone she knew would be understanding.

But she was used to holding her emotions close to her chest, and that type of intimacy wasn't something she could risk.

Physical closeness? Sure.

But opening up emotionally, explaining all the experiences that made her who she was?

No.

And the reality was that the sex she was looking forward to would only last so long. If they were together alone in the villa the entire weekend, she had no doubt the temptation to get to know him better on a personal level, and have him know her, might be overwhelming.

All she needed to remember was that the enjoyment she'd get from sleeping with him would have a time limit, and she always moved on with a clean conscience and no drama.

He'd promised their relationship would fit within those parameters, and there was no way she'd be the one to move the goalpost.

The sun wasn't quite up over the hills when they went down the steps from Piazza Tasso to Marina Piccola in Sorrento, but light already suffused the air, giving the dockside and sea a golden aura. As Massimo bought their tickets, she took a moment to appreciate the sight of him from the back.

Broad shoulders showcased by a lightweight cotton shirt, which also clung enticingly to his strong upper arms.

Lovely butt encased in a buff-colored pair of linen shorts that came with the added bonus of showing off his beautifully muscled calves.

His effortless style was, Kendra thought, a subtle but unmistakable turn-on.

When he turned and caught her staring, she grinned, and Massimo's smile in return did crazy things to her libido, and sent her heart rate soaring. It took more determination to look away than she wanted to admit to.

Most of the people waiting to board seemed local, with only a few backpacked tourists among them.

"Like many places here along the coast, Capri has an influx of seasonal workers at this time of the year," Massimo explained, when Kendra commented as much. "But some find it cheaper to stay on the mainland, and commute by ferry there each day."

"Sure beats the average traffic-clogged drive to work most commuters face," she said, watching with interest as the ferry crew readied the craft. Portside bustle was as familiar to her as the inside of a hospital. "At the very least the views are far better, and the passengers can enjoy them."

Massimo nodded his agreement, but although his lips quirked slightly upward, he didn't smile. There was something different about his demeanor this morning—a tension she wasn't used to seeing—and she couldn't help a little shiver of anticipation. Was he, like her, on tenterhooks knowing they would, finally, be back in each other's arms by the end of the day?

It seemed telling that he hadn't touched her, even casually, that entire morning. Not even once. No hand-holding or guiding touch on her shoulder to usher her into the bus. He'd even sat ever so slightly apart from her on the bus bench and offered no assistance on the stairs down to the dock.

None of these were, on the surface, important, except that she'd noticed in the past those actions were customary. Not just with her, but with everyone.

He was, despite his quiet nature, quite tactile. He would do the hand-on-the-shoulder thing with other staff members when he held the door open for them, as well as taking the *nonne* by the arm to walk them out. Ruffling children's hair, holding Pietro's hand, kissing his *nonna* on both cheeks when he came home, or before he left. All these things seemed to come easily and habitually to him, so his clear reluctance to touch her piqued her curiosity.

They'd taken up a position a little away from the people crowded together waiting for the stevedores to finish loading goods onto the ferry. As soon as the last of the cargo was in place, the gangway was opened and the crowd surged forward, but Massimo didn't move.

Instead, he hung back, waiting for the bulk of the people to board before he waved a hand toward the ferry and said, "Let's go."

"Okay," she replied, but before she stepped forward, she gave in to the irresistible urge that had been building inside to remind him what was to come.

Perhaps even to see, for herself, whether he was as on edge as she was at the thought of them being intimate again.

And definitely to show him that she remembered, with startling clarity, all his erogenous zones, and how to turn him on, sexually.

Using the tips of her fingers, she tickled along his spine, allowing her nails to lightly scrape, knowing he'd feel it clearly through the cotton of his shirt.

And she was rewarded by seeing him shiver.

"Okay," she said again, her voice husky with the longing flowing like a burning river through her veins.

Then she forced her trembling legs to move, before she could forget herself and kiss him senseless, the way she wanted to.

Kendra was playing with fire, and Massimo had no doubt that she was doing it on purpose.

With that one almost innocuous touch, she'd brought it all flooding back.

Memories of her limbs intertwined with his, her gasps and laughter filling his ears. Her surrender to his every caress, and demands that he surrender to hers. Touches and stimulation the likes of which he'd never experienced before, and found mind-blowingly intense.

Her cries of release when she finally, finally gave in to her orgasms.

Recalling those moments, knowing they were about to relive them sometime in the very near future, kept him rooted in place, watching her walk toward the gangway.

Oh, she had no idea what kind of beast she'd awoken when she scratched down his spine.

Watching the enticing sway of her bottom beneath the light pink knit dress she was wearing was enough to make his mouth water.

As he finally got his feet to move, Massimo followed her toward the ferry, and came to a rather frightening realization.

That beast had not really been slumbering at all. It had been lying still, held in control by his will—and hers. But its eyes had been on Kendra the entire time. It had been quivering, waiting for the moment to pounce, wishing and hoping it would get the chance to once more try to devour her with passion.

Getting to know her better hadn't decreased Massimo's desire for her. On the contrary, she'd grown in attractiveness the more he learned. The more he saw of her nature.

The kindness and courtesy toward Nonna and Pietro. Her easy way with patients and coworkers alike. Her adventurous spirit, so in contrast to his own more sedate and carefully planned actions and life.

He didn't want to like her more, or desire her more than he already did. Down that road lay nothing but disappointment and pain. There was no way to avoid the knowledge that not only would she be moving on, as she always did, but also that he—so staid and boring—would never be enough for her. The practical side of his nature demanded he accept that and not become attached, but if he had his way, Kendra Johnson would never forget him, as long as she lived.

And he had the kernel of a plan for making that happen.

He was behind her as she got onboard and immediately made her way to the upper deck, then to the prow of the boat. Silently they stood side by side, her gazing out to sea, while Massimo found himself considering her profile. As the ferry got underway, Kendra lifted her face and he saw her nostrils flare slightly on a deep inward breath, the edges of her lips lifting into a smile.

Was that appreciation for the scene before them, with Capri a rough gem in the distance, and the morning light touching the waves, or pleasure for the power she had over him?

Perhaps she'd forgotten that while she'd been learning his body, he'd been learning hers, and remembered every moment of their time together, which was indelibly etched into his mind?

They were surrounded by people and, he reminded himself, were supposed to be just casual friends, so there was no good opportunity to pay her back—right now.

Instead, he took great pleasure in anticipating his retribution and casually said, "I thought we'd go first to the villa to drop off our things, and then go for a boat tour around the island. It'll be a nice time to visit the Grotta Verde. Then we can decide what you want to see next."

She gave him a sideways look, and a little chuckle, which drove straight through his belly and lit a fire on its way through.

"Sounds great."

Having gotten Sergio's housekeeper's number, Massimo texted her to tell her when they'd be in, and got a reply saying she'd meet them when they docked to hand over the key. This pleased him so much, he found himself grinning.

"What are you smiling about?"

He turned to find Kendra giving him a speculative look, but couldn't erase the smile from his face.

His plan was falling very nicely into place.

"It's a beautiful morning," he said. "And I'm going on an adventure with a beautiful woman. Why wouldn't I be smiling?"

That earned him a snort, and a shake of her head.

"Will there be pirates?" she asked, those bewitching eyes with their slumberous lids gleaming with her amusement. "Or just booty?"

The last part was said in English, and luckily his knowledge of North American popular culture was wide enough for him to understand the double entendre.

If only she knew!

He nodded, holding her gaze and moving a little closer, so that her warmth permeated into the skin of his arm. "Booty, and plundering too," he replied, also in English, and he was enchanted to see color tinge her cheeks.

He'd never seen her blush before.

Shaking her head again, and releasing a breathy laugh, she turned back to watch as Capri grew closer, rising from the sea like a craggy, pastel-bedecked paradise.

Mrs. Casella, Sergio's housekeeper, greeted them with smiles on the dock.

"I've promised to take care of my grandchildren in Anacapri today, so this was the best way to get the key to you," she explained. "And Signor Sergio said I should remind you that the scooters and boat are all at your disposal, should you need them."

They all queued to take the funicular together, but Massimo was glad that Kendra took the lead in carrying the conversation with Mrs. Casella. His mind continued to be preoccupied with thoughts of what was to come.

"The villa is only about a fifteen-minute walk from the Piazzetta," she explained when Kendra asked. "And at this time of the morning it is pleasant indeed. Later it may get quite hot, so my advice is to sightsee now, and then find a nice, shady spot to while away the lunch hours."

"That sounds like a good plan," Kendra told the older lady, as the funicular was coming to a halt.

They said their goodbyes at the Piazzetta, and Massimo took Kendra's hand, as he led her through the main square to a small café. There they had a light breakfast, before once more setting off toward the villa. But he didn't rush, allowing her to browse and look around as they ambled along. It was still too early for many of the shops to be open, but she seemed to enjoy the window-shopping anyway.

As they got closer to Sergio's villa, Massimo saw the way Kendra was looking around, taking in any of the increasingly sumptuous homes visible.

"What did you say your cousin does for a living?" she asked.

"He's an actor, and his husband is a screen and stage writer. They've done very nicely for themselves."

"I'll say," she muttered, just as they approached the gate to Sergio's property, set into a high stone wall that had bougainvillea cascading over it at several points.

While the garden at the back of the house was nice, it was somewhat unassuming, and the house itself was situated in such a manner that the full scope of it was hidden. Massimo led Kendra up the modest staircase, and paused at the top to unlock the door. Once it was open, he stood back for her to precede him into the hall.

She stepped through, then came to a complete stop.

"Crikey," she said, her voice hardly over a whisper, as she took in the opulence of the entryway, with its triple-height ceiling, intricate moldings and massive crystal chandelier. "This is your cousin's house?"

"One of three," he said, easing her farther inside with a hand on the small of her back, and shutting the door behind them. "He and his husband, Robin—who is Scottish—have another in London, and an apartment in New York. Robin does quite a bit of work on Broadway."

Setting down the leather satchel with his clothes on the floor, he eased Kendra's ubiquitous knapsack off her back and placed it next to his bag. Then, taking her hand, he led her through and down the hall to the main sitting room. When he opened the door there, she once more stopped, gaping at the elegant, yet comfortable space.

Sergio was a man who loved both luxury and coziness, and although the preponderance of colorful silk and Persian carpets weren't to Massimo's taste, even he had to admit the effect was striking.

Kendra's gaze traversed the entire room, and her lips were slightly parted, as though in shock. But it was when she saw the view beyond the floor-to-ceiling glass doors that she finally moved, as though drawn to the vista, walking slowly that way.

He strode past her, opening the accordion doors so she could step out onto the wide stone terrace and look around. Even though this was a place for lazy days taking the sun and evenings sipping cocktails, with its overstuffed chairs, marble statues and verdant plants, it wouldn't be out of place in an architectural magazine. Then she was on the move again, her gaze now out at the sea where the Faraglioni jutted arrogantly from the Mediterranean, and she seemed to relax. When she got to the stone parapet surrounding the terrace, her eyes shifted to the formal gardens below, and he heard her draw a deep breath.

"This place is stunning," she said. "So beautiful and overawing. I feel underdressed, as though

I should be wearing a lovely evening gown and diamond tiara."

He hadn't expected such an opening, and yet couldn't resist taking it. Moving behind her, he wrapped one arm around her waist, and twitched her long plait over her shoulder with the other.

"I disagree," he replied, his voice rough with the desire he no longer felt constrained to hide. "I think you are completely overdressed."

CHAPTER THIRTEEN

SHE MELTED. BURNED. All thoughts of not belonging in a place this magnificent fading to nothingness when Massimo wrapped her in his arms from behind.

And if she thought she was the only one who remembered all those erogenous zones they'd discovered that night in Positano, she was very much mistaken.

Massimo's lips were on her nape, causing her head to fall forward, giving him free rein. Then he lightly scraped his teeth across her skin as his mouth slid to the side of her neck, and caused a wave of erotic pleasure to flow like hot wax through her veins.

Her breath rushed, as his hands found their way beneath her dress, caressing up along her thighs.

"I've dreamed of this," he said into her ear, making her shiver with need. "Every night since Positano."

Kendra wanted to tell him she had too, but the intimate admission stuck in her throat.

He didn't seem to need a reply. Indeed, he was too busy driving her crazy, as he sought another of the spots he'd learned turned her on.

For his fingers were tracing around her hip bones, trailing fire in their wake. And his lips now were on the tender skin where neck and shoulder joined.

Her knees wobbled, and she raised her arms to twine around his neck, then gasped as he turned his mouth into the crook of her elbow, tongue swiping against the sensitive flesh.

Oh, yes, his memory was truly excellent, she thought hazily.

She widened her stance, both for balance and in the hopes of enticing him to touch her in the place that truly ached for those thick, skillful fingers, but he ignored her silent plea.

"I want to strip you down right here, in the sunlight, and make love to you all day." His voice was a growl, and Kendra opened her mouth to agree—gleefully—to that idea, but he continued, "But, instead, I think we should find out just how much you truly love anticipation."

His words drove through her, weakening her legs even more.

"What do you mean?" It took so much effort to speak through a throat tight with desire, and there was no disguising the tremble in her voice.

"We will have a morning of sightseeing and foreplay—a boat ride, visiting the Grotta Azzurra, or swim in the Grotta Verde, finding a place to have lunch, whatever you like. We will kiss, and touch, and quietly revel in the anticipation of what will happen when we return here, later, and take pleasure in each other. If you let me, I will take you to the brink and then leave you there, until you tell me it's time for our play to end."

She realized what he meant then, and the sound that came from her lips was unlike any she'd ever heard herself make before.

Primal.

Needy.

Just like the emotions churning in her mind— the passion burning in her belly.

Those big hands slid around to her butt, fingers tracing lines back and forth across the sensitized skin at the very top of her thighs.

How crazy to be so very cranked up with those simple caresses of legs and neck and shoulders. They hadn't kissed. Nor had he touched her any- where most people would consider intimate. Yet, she was already a trembling, yearning mess.

The thought floated into her mind that it was because he *knew*.

Knew what paying attention to those places would do.

And he understood just how much the thought of waiting, anticipating, would turn her on.

Understood, and became complicit in helping her seek—find—that ultimate pleasure.

"But what about you?" she found voice enough to ask, rubbing back against his erection to let him know exactly what she meant.

His chuckle was raw, and his voice little more than a hoarse growl as he replied, "I have been in an almost constant state of need ever since I heard your laughter in the clinic that first day. Another few hours won't cause me to expire."

Turning in his arms, she searched his expression, seeing both the want in his eyes, and the honesty.

Then, as though drawn by a magnetic pull she couldn't resist, her gaze dropped to his mouth.

How had she ever thought his lips too thin? The sensuality of their curves, the visceral recall of how their slick mobility had pleasured her, made another, hotter wave inundate her body.

"Kiss me," she demanded, pressing as close as possible and wrapping her arms around his waist.

He wasted no time acceding, and when their lips met Kendra felt herself surrender in a way she never had before.

Completely. Still caught up in the wonder of a man who seemed to unequivocally accept her just as she was, and didn't hesitate to offer her more than she'd ever dreamed.

"Mmm…" he moaned softly, lifting his lips from hers after a few exhilarating minutes. When he rested his forehead on hers, she sighed, resisting the urge to tug his mouth back to hers. "If we don't stop, my plan will go awry."

"I wouldn't mind," she retorted, waiting to see whether he'd take her up on the invitation, but he shook his head, before straightening.

"Oh, no you don't." His tone was firm, and he shook his head once, for emphasis. "This weekend will be memorable, and I, for one, am looking forward to our day, just as planned. Aren't you?"

There was a definite question in his eyes, despite the obvious desire, and Kendra shivered under that gleaming midnight gaze.

"I am," she admitted, the honest reply drawn from her by his focused attention, and the way his hands cupped her bottom, rhythmically squeezing.

"Then it is decided," Massimo said, in a tone that brooked no argument. "Let me call the marina and have them ready the boat."

Before she could respond, he gave her buttocks one more hard, thrilling squeeze, and then stepped back. Reluctant to let him go, she took her own sweet time, trailing her nails across from the center of his back to his rib cage, and couldn't help laughing when he growled, as though in warning.

Then he turned and disappeared into the villa,

leaving her to sag, almost boneless, against the stones behind her.

Her mind was whirring, while her body hummed with a type of frightening electricity.

How had he reduced her to this state with a few kisses and caresses, and even fewer words?

More importantly, what was this strange sensation burning inside, at the realization that he not only understood her sexual proclivity, but accepted it, wholeheartedly? Had even come up with a plan to push the boundaries into fantasy territory.

He was offering her an experience she hadn't even known she wanted, but now craved with the type of hunger she'd never known before.

Would he touch her, intimately, here, before they left? And when—how, where—would he touch her again, while they were sightseeing?

What an incredibly naughty, arousing, crazy idea, and she had to acknowledge that she was definitely all in on it.

Just the thought of what was to come made her groan, and had another tremor rushing through her body. Her nipples were beaded tight beneath her bra, she knew she was already wet, and wondered if her panties were as soaked as she thought they were.

How was she going to last the morning at this rate?

Had she ever felt this unrestrained before?

She didn't think so.

All her adult life she'd been guarded, in control. What was it about this man, at this time, that broke through those barriers so easily?

That thought took her aback, just a little. Was she conceding too much to Massimo? Giving him too much access into her head?

Shouldn't she at least try to claw back some of her autonomy, before she lost herself completely in the experience?

But when it occurred to her what she wanted to do next, it wasn't driven by those fears, but by a totally different thought.

Moving over to one of the plush loungers scattered around the terrace, she sat on the edge, letting the distant murmur of Massimo's deep voice wash over her. He was doing something for her that she'd never expected. Offering her an experience in pleasure beyond any she'd been gifted before.

She wanted it to be as good for him as it would be for her, and delayed gratification was her kink, not his.

His voice came closer, and she heard him bidding whoever was on the other end of the line goodbye, just as he stepped back onto the terrace.

"The manager of the marina where Sergio's boat is docked says it will be ready for us within the hour," he said.

"Oh, good. Then we have time."

Perhaps it was the timbre of her voice, or the expression on her face, that had him stopping in his tracks, his searching gaze bringing heat to her face—and other places too.

"Time for what?"

She beckoned him closer with a crooked finger. "Come here, and I'll show you."

For an instant she thought he'd refuse, and even when he approached it was slowly, almost hesitantly.

When he was within arm's length, she smiled up at him, as she reached for his belt.

"Wait." Those lovely large hands reached down to hold hers.

"Why?"

"You don't have to—"

Kendra laughed, and shook her head. "Of course I don't *have* to, but I *want* to."

And when she wriggled out of his grasp and set about undoing his fly, then the buttons of his shirt, he didn't put up any further argument, only exhaled with a hiss as he stepped out of his shorts. Reaching down, he put one hand on her shoulder, while the other reached for her plait and wrapped it around his fingers.

She didn't hold back, and didn't let him either. Taking her time, savoring the taste, and scent, and texture of him, she took him to the edge, and held him there for a long moment. Growling her name, Massimo tugged on her hair. She set him free, so as to look up at him and laugh with pleasure. His face was tight, lips drawn back, two slashes of red staining his cheeks, his breathing ragged.

"You need to stop, now."

"No." She licked her lips, hoping he could see just how much she was aroused by what they were doing. "You need to let go, and give me what I want."

Still he hesitated and, held by her hair, unable to move toward him, Kendra stayed motionless. Looking up at him, she silently willed him to take a chance, to break out of whatever bounds were keeping him from accepting what she was offering.

If he couldn't trust her with his body—with his pleasure—could she trust him with hers the way she wanted to?

Something flashed in his eyes, and if she didn't know better, she'd have thought it was fear, but before she could properly analyze it, he gave in, and loosened his grip.

And she had only a moment to let out one huff of laughter before she took him back between her lips, and not long after, to ecstasy.

His legs were trembling, and he braced himself on her shoulders. As his breathing grew slower, his fingers loosened, and Kendra laughed softly.

"I enjoyed that," she said, just in case he didn't realize. "Can we do it again later?"

A strained chuckle was the reply, and Massimo slowly straightened.

What a gorgeous sight he was, naked except for his unbuttoned shirt, which, hanging open, only accentuated his thick, muscular trunk. Reaching up, she ran her hand over his chest, grazing one nipple, before following the line of hair that arrowed down to his navel.

He held her hand, and shook his head.

"My turn."

Heat spiked from her chest down into her belly, and her internal muscles gave a sweet little spasm.

"I'm not sure that would be wise," she warned huskily, although just then the thought of abandoning his luscious plan didn't seem such a bad thing. "I'm pretty much on the edge of coming right now."

He smiled, and the feral edge to it caused another ripple of arousal deep in her abdomen.

"I'll be careful. It is far too early in the day for your first orgasm."

Caught in his gaze, her body vibrating and hot, surrounded by the lush plants and growing warmth of the beautiful setting, something broke free inside. Something that had everything and nothing to do with lust. Everything and nothing to do with physical need. A sensation—an emotion—that bade her to give in.

Urged her to trust.

To push aside the sudden spurt of apprehension and open herself to the moment—to Massimo—without reservation.

But, as though mirroring Massimo's reluctance of before, she hesitated.

It felt familiar—the fear. The sensation of a turning point, or the solid ground she'd built for herself shifting, ever so slightly, beneath her feet.

Yet, she'd never shied away from any challenge, and this was, indisputably, an adventure for the ages.

So she laughed, although it burned her throat slightly on the way out, and put her hands behind her, so she half reclined on the lounger.

"Do your worse. Or your best," she said, in English, too fuzzy-brained to find the right words in Italian. Taunting him a little and using bravado to keep from showing him her uncertainty.

"Always my best," he replied before, with a move almost too graceful for a man of his size, he sank to his knees, and pulled her closer with a tug. After he pulled down her panties and nudged her legs apart, he paused, looking down. She felt his gaze on her flesh like a touch, and trembled in reaction. "Only the best, for you."

Then he slid his hands under her bum, and lifted her while he dipped his head, and Kendra was completely, inexplicably, lost.

CHAPTER FOURTEEN

As he steered the motorboat out of the marina, Massimo was feeling extremely pleased with himself, if still a little shaken. The encounter at the villa between Kendra and him had been erotic beyond belief, and the almost drunken look on her face before they left had made his ego inflate to ridiculous proportions.

No woman had ever made him feel the way she did.

Bold.

In charge.

But also vulnerable, knowing he was with a woman who possessed a self-assurance he could only ever wish for. Yet, with her it was easy to assume an air of confidence, and to allow himself to simply act rather than analyze every move he made, in case it was wrong.

With her he was comfortable in his own skin.

Perhaps too comfortable and confident.

After their tryst, she'd gone to change into her

swimsuit and come back out wearing a pair of shorts. Massimo had shaken his head.

"Go and change back into your sundress," he'd said, surprising them both by the demand in his voice. "I want to be able to touch you whenever I want today."

Color flooded her cheeks and her lips had parted in silent shock. Then, without a word, she'd turned around and gone to do what he bade.

He'd never in his life been so commanding to a woman, and of all the women he'd been with, Kendra was the last one he'd have thought would comply without question.

Or without telling him to go to hell.

They were out on the open water now, but he kept the vessel at idle speed, taking the opportunity to look over his shoulder at Kendra, wondering if she were upset. Once she'd secured the line the dockhand had tossed to her, she'd settled into one of the seats behind him, rather than sit in the chair beside his.

She was half-sprawled on the bench seat, her head back, exposing the lovely long line of her throat. Her sunglasses were perched on the top of her head, and her eyes were closed.

"Are you sleeping back there?" he called, over the sound of the motor.

She half opened her eyes and smiled at him.

"No, just appreciating the moment, and wondering if this deprivation thing is really right for me. I'm so revved up I could explode just from the vibrations of the engine."

He loved when she spoke like that, so frankly sexual and open about her feelings, although it made him a little crazy too.

"Don't talk like that when I'm supposed to be concentrating on what I'm doing," he warned. "Or I'll have to come over there and make sure that when that explosion happens, I'm the one who causes it."

She pulled her glasses down and put them on with a chuckle, which just made his reawakening lust spike a bit higher.

"Oh, believe me, I'm holding out for that too."

"Come and sit next to me." He patted the seat beside the pilot's chair. "I want everyone we pass to see the beautiful woman with me."

Another deep, husky laugh was the only answer he got, but she got up and moved to sit beside him, and Massimo felt his shoulders relax.

"This really is a lovely boat. The teak is amazing."

He grinned. "Lucky for me, our grandfather made sure all of his grandchildren learned three things. How to swim, how to know when a lemon was ready to be picked and how to operate a boat safely. Otherwise Sergio would never offer to allow me to take his baby out of the marina."

"I don't blame him. She's a thing of beauty." She stretched, and then, in a purely unselfconscious way, ran her hands over her belly and hummed. "What a glorious day."

He wanted to ask her if it was the weather making her say so, or if he had some hand in helping her feel that way, but the words stuck in his chest.

Then she looked over at him, and smiled in such a way he wished he could see her eyes instead of just his own reflection in her sunglasses. But even thus hindered, his body tightened, and he found himself smiling back.

He opened up the throttle a bit more, and started west along the coast, pointing out landmarks to her as they went.

"Would you like to go inside the Grotta Azzurra?" he asked, as they meandered along the northern coast. "It's not far from here. We can anchor and hire one of the rowers to take us in."

"I would. It's one of the things I was told I really should do while here."

Of course, Massimo had been in the sea cave many times before—had even gone back in the evening, after the tourists were gone, and swam in it—but now he was looking forward to showing it to Kendra. In a strange way, he felt as though she understood his love of the Amalfi Coast and all its beauty, even though it would never be as appealing to her as it was to him.

She'd seen so many places, and lived such an adventurous life, there was nothing here to hold her interest for long.

The thought made him angry and even more determined that once she moved on, she would never forget him. Steering the boat farther out to sea for about a mile, he set the engine to idle. While there were a few boats in the distance, they were, for all intents and purposes, alone, and he turned to face her, resting his hand on her knee.

Kendra was watching him, and she licked her lips, then visibly swallowed.

He didn't speak, not trusting himself to say the correct thing just then. Instead, he reached out and took off her glasses, tossing them onto the dashboard. Spinning her chair toward him, he stepped forward, and kissed her—hard.

There was no hesitation in the way she kissed him back. Tangling her tongue with his, then sucking on his lower lip, the motion bringing back vivid memories of the way she'd taken him into her mouth earlier.

Reaching up beneath her skirt, he found the edge of her swimsuit, and ran his finger lightly along the elastic circling her leg. There was a spot, just about there…

"Mmm," she moaned into his mouth, her back arching so her breasts rubbed his chest.

He drew back, bending to nip at her neck.

"I want to touch you." He said it into her ear, knowing it wasn't as sensitive as his were, yet that nevertheless she never failed to react when he spoke right into one, and was rewarded when she shivered.

"Do anything you want," she said, spreading her thighs, her head dropping back against the seat. "I give you permission."

"Anything?"

Her eyes were dark, yet sparked hot, her drooping lids giving her an even more sultry expression than usual.

"Anything."

He pulled her to her feet, and, bunching the hem in either hand, tugged her dress off over her head. She was wearing a two-piece suit, and he was ridiculously excited to note the top had a zipper down the front.

He made good use of it, baring her full breasts with their dark nipples now tightly furled.

Cupping them, he rubbed his thumbs over those enticing peaks, circling and then pinching them between his fingers. Entranced by the goose bumps that fanned out across her chest, he bent, and licked at her flesh. Starting at one peak, he drew patterns on her skin with his tongue until she laughed that breathy, sexy laugh, and her thighs tightened around his.

Without breaking contact between his mouth

and her breast, he reached between them and cupped between her thighs, hearing her muffled cry of pleasure.

He didn't dare go beneath the cloth, knowing he wouldn't stop until she came. This game they were playing was much harder than he could have ever expected. It was only by putting her wants and needs ahead of his own selfish desires that he could restrain himself.

He wanted to sink his fingers into the velvet-wet heat he knew awaited inside her. Use lips and tongue on her clitoris until she cried for completion. Sheath himself inside her, and drive home until they both exploded and stars danced behind his eyes.

Unable to resist, he told her all those things, his hand motionless on her mound, the other tugging at a nipple. Kendra groaned his name, her hips pumping against his palm, her fingers tangled into his hair, holding his head against her neck.

Realizing how frantic her movements were becoming, he drew his hand away, and reached up to free himself from her grasping fingers.

"There," he said, pulling her top back into place, but not before one last kiss on a nipple. "That's enough for now, I think."

He tried to sound factual, even casual, but it was impossible with his heart trip-hammering and his lungs barely able to pull in enough air.

When she huffed out a breathy passion-struck sound of amusement, it almost made him forget his promise, and he had to force himself to turn back to the controls, while Kendra fixed her top.

Kendra pulled the two sides of her bikini top together and tried to insert the end of the zipper into the tab. It was extremely difficult when her fingers were trembling, clumsy with arousal.

Her entire body felt sensitized, almost painful, and yet she didn't have a moment's regret for the pact they'd made.

She'd never felt more alive.

Massimo was turning the boat back toward land, going slowly, probably waiting for her to complete her chore, and it gave her the opportunity to examine his profile at her leisure.

There again was that slash of color on his cheek, the firming of his jaw speaking to his own unsatisfied need. He glanced at her and caught her staring, just as she got the zipper going.

"That was a close one," she told him frankly. "I almost lost it."

His nostrils flared slightly as he took a deep breath. "I realized."

"It was your fault, you know." He glanced at her out of the corner of his eye, his brow raised, as though in question. "I was fine until you started telling me all the things you want to do to me."

"Should I not do that?"

There was no amusement in the question, and she realized he was serious.

"Actually, I loved it." A chuckle broke free, borne on the sharpness of her need, and genuine amusement. "A little too much."

"Perhaps it makes you feel as I do when you laugh while we are intimate."

Genuinely surprised, she asked, "What?"

Massimo shrugged, the corners of his lips lifting. "Your laughter makes me hard, and when we are making love, it makes me lose all control if I am not careful."

"I'll have to remember that," she said, amused and in a weird way pleased.

"Actually, it makes me hard all the time, for it reminds me of the time we were in bed. When I would caress you and, finding a place you particularly liked, you'd laugh."

Why did that touch her, make a little glow start in her chest and spread slowly out from there?

Perhaps because in the past she'd been told her laughter was too loud, too robust, unladylike, and should be better controlled. Knowing it had that kind of effect on Massimo was revelatory.

But that was a fact she would keep to herself. She was even unable to tease him about it, knowing she couldn't pull that off without revealing at least some of what she was feeling.

Afraid he'd see the sheen of tears in her eyes, she quickly bent to pick up her dress and tug it on. Then, as added security, she grabbed her glasses and stuck them on her face, suddenly needing the separation they gave her from his all-too-knowing gaze.

"Next stop, Grotta Azzurra," he said, blithely unaware of how he'd rocked her to the core, and left her far more than just physically shaken.

"Carry on," she replied, pleased when her voice came out almost normal.

Hopefully he'd put the little tremor in it down to the desire still shimmering under her skin, where it mixed with that warm, tender sensation he'd stirred up.

Damn him!

The Blue Grotto lived up to its hype, a fact that totally blew Kendra's mind. There were so many tourist destinations that failed to be as beautiful as they were advertised to be, but there was no denying the sea cave was completely mesmerizing.

First was the unconventional way they had to enter—lying down in a small rowboat, as the oarsman pulled them in with hand-over-hand tugs on a rope through the low, narrow mouth of the cave. And then, inside...

Kendra gasped at the almost unbelievable blue

of the water, which was, the oarsman told her, caused by light coming in through an underwater aperture. It was almost like being in a sea of blue fluorescent animals, made even more sublime by the flashing reflections on the walls.

Without conscious thought, she reached for Massimo's hand, and he twined his fingers with hers. The sensation felt so shockingly right, so intimate, she almost pulled away, but couldn't bring herself to do it.

It was an all-too-brief stop, and after a few minutes they were rowing back toward the entrance, their oarsman no doubt eager to collect another fare from the excursion boat anchored outside. But when one of the other oarsmen started to sing, Massimo asked him to wait, just for a minute, so they could listen, and for the second time in the day Kendra found herself close to tears.

The sheer beauty of the cave, and the singing, and having her hand held so very tenderly was almost too much to bear.

Thankfully, she was able to pull herself together by the time they got back out into the sunlight, and busying herself with pulling the anchor also gave her a little more breathing room.

Farther along, Massimo pointed out the site of a Roman ruin, then a series of forts along the western coast. Although he seemed little different from how he was the rest of the day, Kendra felt a strange atmosphere building between them, making her edgy.

It was, she reasoned, the sexual tension he'd so carefully cultivated, yet even to herself that didn't ring quite true.

Oh, there was no doubt she was still on a sexual high, irrespective of those moments in Grotta Azzurra that had shaken her so emotionally. But, even so, what had started out as an escapade—an arousing lark—had somehow started to morph into something different, and she wasn't sure what that something was.

Realizing she'd been mooning over his profile once again, she tore her gaze away and lifted her face to the sun. The sea breeze washed over her skin, and she inhaled deeply. It should have brought her peace, the way the ocean always did, but today that calm eluded her.

"I thought we could stop for lunch at a beachside restaurant near the Faraglioni." Massimo's voice pulled her out of her reverie, and her gaze was drawn back to him. Unable to resist, she reached out to brush the hair back from his forehead, and was rewarded with a smile. "But if you're not yet hungry, we could stop for a swim at the Grotta Verde first."

What she really wanted was to drag him back to his cousin's villa and have her wicked way with him, in the hopes that once that was over this sense of being on a tilt-a-whirl would go away. Telling him that, though, would be far too revealing, so she smiled instead.

"I'd like a swim, I think. It's getting quite hot now, even with the sea breeze."

He nodded, and sent her a sideways glance that raised the simmering desire beneath her skin at least ten degrees.

"There will be others in the grotto, but even so I will touch you again. I can't keep my hands off you for much longer."

And the huff of delight that broke from her throat had little to do with amusement, and a lot to do with need.

CHAPTER FIFTEEN

MASSIMO WAS TRUE to his word, although he was extremely discreet in how he caressed her while they frolicked in the emerald waters of Grotta Verde. Now that he knew she also liked when he told her all the things he longed to do to her, he used his voice as well as his touch to turn her on.

And the list of sensual, sexual actions he came up with surprised even himself. He'd always thought of himself as conventional—even dull— in his needs, but the beast Kendra unleashed in him was anything but staid.

He wanted her in every way he could think of. Nothing off-limits, unless she was unwilling, and she didn't seem averse to anything he suggested, which made him even wilder with desire.

Keeping their association on a strictly carnal level wasn't easy, however. His curiosity kept growing apace with his passion. Yet, as he discovered, getting her to talk more about herself, especially her earlier life, wasn't easy.

After they'd swum back to the boat, and he was

drying off, he saw her once more turn her face up to the sun, and inhale, taking in the briny air, a smile lighting her face.

Something about her posture resonated with him, and Massimo found himself saying, "You really love the sea, don't you? I remember the first time I saw you, looking out over the bay at Spiaggia Tordigliano. I thought you looked as though you wanted to scoop the water up in your arms and hug it."

Her smile widened, and she sent him a sideways glance. "It sounds poetic when you say it that way, but yes, that's exactly how I feel whenever I see the sea. I inherited the love of it from my father."

Without thought, he asked, "And what did you inherit from your mother?"

All signs of pleasure dropped away from her face, and her lips twisted for a moment as she shrugged.

"I have no idea. I've never met her, and never will."

His heart stuttered, and he said the first thing that came to mind. "Is she deceased?"

Another shrug, but while now she tried to smile, he saw through it. That was the way she looked when she was in retreat, but didn't want anyone to know.

"I don't know that either." There was a moment of hesitation, and he thought that would be the end of the conversation, but then she sighed. "She was a foreign grad student at the university Dad attended. They had an affair and when she got pregnant he offered to marry her, but she wasn't interested. According to my aunt, she told him her family would never accept him because he was Black, and wouldn't accept me either. So she hid the pregnancy from her family, had me and then took off back to Argentina."

Dumbfounded, he shook his head. "Astounding. She has no idea of the joy she's missed, by not knowing you."

Kendra glanced at him out of the corner of her eye, then turned away, so he couldn't see her face.

"It's no big deal. I learned to accept it a long time ago."

But he believed that statement just as much as he'd believed that distancing smile she'd given him just moments before.

Then, before he could persist with the conversation, she said, "Now I'm definitely hungry. It's been a long time since breakfast."

Without further comment, he started the motor, and they continued along the south coast. Restless now, not with unsated desire but with anger at her mother's defection, he opened up the throttle, putting the powerful boat through its paces. As they cut through the waves, he glanced over at Kendra and her smile of pleasure eased some of the pain around his heart.

No matter how difficult his home life had ever been, at least his parents were always around. Despite his father making his disappointment with Massimo clear, and both parents so focused on each other it sometimes felt their children were an afterthought, at least he'd had his grandparents' support. He may have felt lost in the shuffle, something of an outsider because of his retiring nature, but there had never been a time when Massimo had felt truly alone.

How had Kendra managed, growing up without her mother, losing her father when she was ten?

And what impact had her mother's defection had on her development?

It all just made him want to know more.

Reminding himself that she would be gone from his life within a short time reined in his curiosity. Seeing her retreat from the conversation warned him that she wouldn't appreciate his prying any further.

But hearing her talk about the exciting aspects of her life would help him to remember the vast difference between them, and squelch any inclination he may have to get closer to her, emotionally.

They anchored near the seaside restaurant he'd

202 ONE-NIGHT FLING IN POSITANO

"One of the ways they tried to help the kids in the program—many of whom came from really disadvantaged circumstances—was to find mentors, and I was paired with a doctor whose family had moved to Canada from the Caribbean." She shook her head, her gaze growing distant, as though remembering it all. "Dr. Amie really turned my life around. She's a real Renaissance woman, you know? She was interested in everything, from music to nature, other cultures too, and, of course, the sciences. She'd take me to museums and concerts, even to the ballet and opera, but also got me into reading, and art appreciation—everything. Through her I started to realize there was a great big world out there, waiting to be explored."

"She sounds wonderful," he said, as Kendra paused to take another sip of her wine. "I'm surprised she didn't encourage you to become a doctor."

Kendra laughed. "I think she secretly wanted me to become one, especially when I told her that was what my father had wanted to do too, but she wasn't into pushing anything on me. What she did was broaden my horizons, then got me thinking about what I wanted, and how I could get there. The future really wasn't something I thought too much about at that point, you know? But she encouraged me to keep my grades chosen, and a dory came to ferry them ashore. Once they were seated at a table overlooking the famous rocks and had ordered, he leaned back in his chair, and said, "I've been curious about how you ended up in the army."

She smiled, and seemed to relax. He hadn't noticed how tense she'd been since their earlier conversation until her shoulders dropped at his question.

"It was a matter of finding a way to do what I wanted to, which was travel," she replied. "That's the simplified version of the story, anyway."

"What's the complicated version?"

He held his breath, wondering if Kendra would retreat again, but saw no change in her demeanor, and breathed out as she put down the glass she'd been sipping from and replied.

"Well, when I was about fourteen, I went to live with my aunt in an area adjacent to a pretty notorious neighborhood in Toronto. I started hanging out with a group of friends she didn't approve of but, having hit the rebellious stage, I kept seeing them anyway. Then, one of the group got arrested for shoplifting, and my aunt decided I needed something else to do after school, and enrolled me in a program at the community center."

Her smile widened, as though the memory was a good, rather than bad, one.

up, explaining that was the way to keep my options open and then, finally, one day she sat me down and asked what I wanted to do when I left school."

"And you told her you wanted to travel the world."

She nodded, her eyelids lowering for a moment, so he couldn't see the expression in her eyes.

"And she asked what I planned to do to make that happen." Kendra chuckled, and tucked a stray strand of hair that had escaped her plait behind her ear. "Needless to say, I hadn't given that a lot of thought, and shrugged the question off. But the next time we were together, she forced me to think it through. Would I want to go to college, and get a degree that would enable me to travel? Could I become a travel writer, or agent? How else could I finance this peripatetic life I wanted? After going over all the options, I figured it would be best to join the military, and train to be a nurse. Then I wouldn't have student loans to pay off, and I'd also get to travel while in the military too."

For an instant his mind flashed on an image of his own carefree time at school—difficult, because he'd chosen medicine, but not because he'd had to work his way through, or think about tuition.

His respect for Kendra, for the way she'd risen above her childhood and made her dreams come true, on her own terms, rose to new heights.

"So volunteering for the army was a means to an end, as was nursing?"

"I guess so." She chuckled, the sweet, warm sound wrapping around him. "Although I chose the career carefully, not just at random. Dr. Amie made sure of that. For a while it was a toss-up between nursing and culinary school, but after doing a volunteer stint at a hospital, I was hooked."

Surprised, he cocked an eyebrow at her. "You like to cook?"

"Love it. I started fooling around in the kitchen, making meals for my cousins and myself when we got home from school, and it grew from there." A thoughtful, almost sad look crossed her face. "It's the one thing I really miss when I'm on the road." Then her expression lightened. "But whenever I go back to Canada, my cousin Koko makes sure I cook for her. She says she doesn't have many good, home-cooked meals while I'm away, but makes sure she doesn't let her mother hear her say it."

And as they laughed together, Massimo was left once more considering just how much he admired her, and wondering why it all made him want her even more.

* * *

What was it about Massimo that made him so easy to speak to—to bare parts of herself she rarely, if ever, shared with anyone?

Settling into the small dinghy that would row them back to the boat, Kendra avoided looking at Massimo, feeling raw. Exposed.

Instead she looked up at the majestic rock formations jutting from the sea and then, as though unable to help it, at the outline of the villa's roof, visible from this position. Massimo had pointed it out to her earlier, and she'd shivered, imagining getting back there—finally experiencing the release she'd been craving all day.

Now, staring up at the house, she knew she was ready. More than ready, although that knowledge came with another spurt of fear.

It was supposed to be a no-strings-attached situation, and it was usually the men she slept with who tried to change the script. Now it was she who was battling against a connection she'd felt from the first moment she saw him, months ago at the beach.

She didn't believe in instant attraction, really. Or even less love at first sight. But there was no escaping the fact that the draw she felt toward Massimo—both physically and emotionally—was stronger than she knew how to handle.

Already she had to admit to herself that sleeping with him again was probably the worst idea she'd had in a long time, from a peace-of-mind standpoint, but it was too late to back out now. Not that he would try to force her. In fact, she knew without a doubt, if she told him she'd changed her mind, he would immediately accept her decision.

No. The real problem was that she wanted him, and all that he had to offer, too much to resist.

She'd take this weekend, and all he had to give here on Capri, then figure it out afterward. Make the hard decisions.

But as she looked up at the rocky coastline, and breathed in the salty air, she finally admitted she'd be leaving a piece of herself here when she left. And, for the first time in a long, long time, the thought of moving on brought no joy.

Back onboard, Massimo started the engine while she weighed anchor and, once they were underway and she'd neatly stowed the line, she moved aft to where he sat at the controls. Sliding in behind him, she leaned her chin on his shoulder, and turned her head so her lips almost touched his ear.

"I'm ready," she whispered, and felt him shudder. "No more stops. No more waiting. Let's go back to the villa."

He didn't reply, just opened the throttle, and the boat jumped up on a plane as it carved through the water. Grabbing the back of his chair to keep her balance, Kendra laughed, and ran the tip of her tongue along the edge of Massimo's ear, earning a growl that was clearly audible above the engine noise.

Then she realized that instead of following the coastline as it curved north, he was heading out into open water, and her heart began to hammer. Far out from land, he put the boat in Neutral, and turned to her.

All around them lay the glorious blue of the ocean, Capri just a gray-and-green lump in the distance. Here there was just the low hum of the idling engine and the cries of gulls feeding a little way off.

Massimo's eyelids drooped, and his lips tightened for a moment before he spoke.

"You're ready for our game to end?"

"Yes." She nodded in emphasis.

"I'm not sure I am," he replied, still seated, making no effort to move, or to take her into his arms. "At least, not in the way I envisioned."

It never occurred to her that he might be having second thoughts too, and her heart plummeted at his words.

She lifted her chin, determined to maintain her poise. Not let him see her fear and disappointment.

"You've changed you mind about us sleeping together?"

As hard as she'd tried to keep her voice steady, it still came out weaker than she'd have liked, but when Massimo shook his head, the rush of relief she felt turned her knees to jelly.

"Not at all. I feel as though if I don't make love to you, I will... I don't know what I'll do, but it wouldn't be good."

Tilting her head to the side, she asked, "Then why are we here, instead of racing back to the marina?"

He didn't answer her question, but gestured with his chin to the bench seat.

"Go. Sit."

Oh, why did she turn to mush when he became demanding? She wasn't sure there was another man alive who could boss her around this way and get away with it, much less have her almost mindlessly comply.

But it was Massimo, and so she turned obediently and took a seat.

By the time he got up and came to stand in front of her, she was trembling all over, and her toes were curled against the deck. When he sank to his knees, another of those crazy, untamed sounds broke from her throat.

Massimo's hands were on her outer thighs, and he looked up at her.

"I don't know what it is you do to me, Kendra." His voice was low, rough, and the sound of it seemed to vibrate into her skin. "I know myself to be a staid man—you might even say dull—but around you I become..." He hesitated, seemingly searching for the right word. "Wild. Like an animal. Operating on instinct and primal needs alone."

Surprised, she huffed. "The man who whispered into my ear all those incredibly sexy ideas about what we can do in bed is anything but staid. Or dull."

He shrugged. "You prove my point. I have been called *tedious. Too careful. Boring.* And before meeting you I would have agreed. Now, I hardly know myself."

She sat up straight, then leaned forward to lift that wayward lock of hair that always flopped onto his forehead.

"The people who called you those things clearly didn't know you well. The man who went into that damaged house was almost ridiculously bold and daring. And the way you ride a scooter and drive a boat tells me there is a daredevil just under your quiet surface, waiting to bust out." Then she leaned closer yet. "And the man who has given me a day that can only be described as fantastical, who's kept me so aroused there were times I could hardly function normally, is anything but tedious."

Reaching up, he pulled off her sunglasses and

tossed them aside, searching her gaze, as if trying to see if she meant what she'd said.

"You've brought that out in me," he replied, and his hands slid up under her dress. When his fingers slipped into the waistband of her bikini bottoms, she instinctively lifted her hips.

"Maybe," she said, forcing the words out through her suddenly dry throat. "But I didn't create that in you, and couldn't bring it out if it wasn't already there."

He grunted in reply, apparently too busy pulling her bottoms off to say anything more.

"What are you planning?" she asked, not liking the suspense and wondering what his change of tactics actually entailed.

He looked up, holding her gaze, and in the bright sunlight, out here on the water, golden lights seemed to gleam in the depths of his eyes.

"I want to make you crazy," he said, as though that would be something new. As though he hadn't been doing just that all day. "And then I want to watch you lose control. Then, when we get back to the villa, I want to do it all over again. And again. And again."

As he spoke, he parted her thighs, and slid his hands up until they rested on that sensitive area just below her hip bone.

Kendra gasped, pulling a short hot breath into

her lungs, and spread her legs even wider, urging him on.

Massimo slowly parted her labia with his thumbs, and Kendra arched, feeling the slick slide of his flesh against hers.

Then the sweet, erotic torture began, lasting until she was begging, *begging* him for surcease, and her laughter and cries of release joined the raucous shrieks of the gulls.

CHAPTER SIXTEEN

KENDRA WATCHED CAPRI dwindling into the distance behind the ferry with almost heart-wrenching regret.

The three days in Capri with Massimo had flown by, filled with laughter, fun and mind-blowing lovemaking. Massimo had taken her to heights of pleasure unlike anything she'd experienced before. The knowledge he'd gleaned about her body, his way of taking what she'd always considered a silly predilection and elevating it—and her—to a whole new level of eroticism had turned her inside out.

It should be enough.

Physically she was sated, but mentally, emotionally, she craved more.

More closeness, like the evenings, after dinner, when they'd shared a lounge chair out on the terrace at the villa, sipping wine and talking. Leaning back against Massimo's broad chest, having his arm around her waist, feeling him drop kisses

onto her temple, had brought Kendra an inde-
scribable sense of peace.

She'd wanted to stay there forever, never having to move out of that warm embrace. Wanted to
tell him everything there was to know about her,
learn everything about him, so that the bond she
already felt could grow into something strong,
and true.

Every time she looked at him, even in the most
banal of situations, her heart skipped a beat, and
a strange, nonsexual warmth threw her mind into
disarray.

It was, in a word, *inexplicable*.

Sex she was used to, and was quite happy to
indulge in. Even a loose type of friendship was
typical of her encounters with men, but that was
where she usually drew the line.

Yearning for emotional closeness and support,
longing for a relationship built on more than lust,
was verboten.

There was no place for any of it in her life.

Or is there?

The whispered thought wafted through her
brain and refused to go away, even when she
pushed against its allure.

Massimo Bianchi was a man who had a solid
place in the world, she reminded herself, while
she was, in her own word, a vagabond. Settling
down in one place wasn't in the cards for her—a

fact she'd accepted long ago. Only by moving, by exploring, could she feel complete.

She'd tried staying in one place after she'd left the armed forces, but the restlessness wouldn't leave her, until her apartment—her life—became stifling. She truly believed she was born to rove, to seek in far-flung and distant places so as to find the meaning of her existence.

Even if Massimo were interested in trying to build something with her, could she take the chance that she wouldn't be able to deliver what he needed, long term?

Especially when she factored Pietro, and even Mrs. Bianchi too, into the equation, the risk didn't seem worth it. The little boy needed a solid, loving, stable home, and Kendra knew she wasn't capable of delivering one.

Or if she attempted to, it might not last.

How could she risk making the attempt, letting all the residents of Agriturismo Villa Giovanna get used to having her around, only to realize it had been a mistake to stay? Her heart ached at the thought of how Pietro would probably feel— abandoned, unlovable—and how the experience may set him back.

It wasn't a chance she wanted to take.

Some people just weren't meant to remain forever in one place, and she was one of that wandering tribe. Why hurt others when it was completely avoidable?

"Everything okay?"

Caught up in her less-than-happy thoughts, Kendra started, not realizing Massimo had returned from the commissary and was standing beside her.

Pushing her sunglasses more firmly up on her nose, she sent him a smile, even though it took a huge effort.

"Of course," she replied, accepting the bottle of water he held out for her, and opening it. "Just woolgathering."

She'd said the last bit in English, unable to think of the Italian equivalent, and Massimo turned to lean on the railing so he was looking directly at her. Something about his expression, the way he seemed to focus in on her face so intently, set alarm bells ringing in her head.

"I've noticed," he said slowly, "you usually only use English when you're upset. Your Italian is really exemplary otherwise."

She forced a laugh. "I'm not upset. How could I be, after the hedonistic weekend we just had?"

Massimo didn't reply and, as she took a sip of water, Kendra mentally patted herself on the back, glad to have reminded them both what the weekend had truly been about.

Sex.

Incredible, heart-stopping, almost-break-the-bed, blow-off-the-top-of-her-head sex, but just sex, nonetheless.

Even if she'd just finished berating herself for thinking otherwise.

Massimo took a long drink from his bottle, his gaze still trained on her face. After he'd swallowed, he said, "I would like to have such a weekend with you again. Or even just a night, here or there, if that is all we can arrange."

Kendra's heart stuttered, and she bit the inside of her cheek, so as not to agree immediately. Wouldn't it be better to start letting things cool down from now, rather than continue on what had become, for her, an increasingly slippery slope?

"I'm not sure how that would work out," she finally replied. "I don't want your grandmother to get the wrong idea, which she will, if we keep running off together."

He snorted. "Nonna may be old-fashioned, but she's well aware of the way modern relationships work. She's not the type to assume that if we are sleeping together, it means anything more than that."

Another revelation, as Kendra—who never gave a fig what anyone thought of her—realized that in Mrs. Bianchi's case, she actually did care. Losing the older lady's esteem and friendship was not something she wanted to do.

"Maybe so, but why take the chance of giving her the wrong impression? Like most grandmothers, I'm sure she wants to see you settle down. It would be worse for you in the long term if she even has the thought that it might be a possibility, and then I leave."

"Perhaps you're right," he said, but there was a note in his voice she didn't know how to interpret. "Have you decided where you're going next—when you leave Minori?"

She was the one who'd brought up leaving, so why did her hackles rise because he'd mentioned it too, as though already eager to see the back of her?

Even knowing she was being silly, her voice was cool when she replied, "Not yet. I have out a few feelers in other parts of Europe, but I'm actually considering going back to Canada for a while. It's been a few years since I saw my family, and I know I can pick up work there, easily."

"You had said you wanted to see more of Italy. I thought perhaps you'd travel here for a while before you left."

How on earth did he remember that?

"It depends on how quickly I need to find a new position." Now she was just making stuff up, on the fly. She always had a nice contingency fund in place, just so as *not* to have to rush from job to job. "I've also been thinking of going to

Spain, although nurses aren't on the shortage occupation list, so I'd have to find something else to do. I hold a teaching certificate, so that might be an option."

The last bit was totally off the cuff, since she hadn't looked at the Spanish government website in a few years.

"Well, you have a little time to make a decision. Just under two months, right?"

He'd been keeping track of the time she had left too, then. Was he counting the days they had left together, or how quickly it was he'd be rid of her?

"Seven weeks. Which isn't very much when you think about all that goes into moving around like I do. Hell, when I first thought of coming here, and applied through the program, it took me a year to put it all together, not counting the eighteen months I was stuck in Dubai. I'm glad you reminded me that I need to make some solid plans. If I don't start now, leaving might turn out to be more expensive than I want."

But, as she changed the subject, she suspected that no matter what plans she made, the cost of leaving Minori was already more than she wanted to pay.

Not in cash, but in emotional currency.

As the ferry drew closer to Positano, Massimo led Kendra toward the front of the ferry, then excused himself, telling her he would return momentarily. Walking to the other side of the boat, he leaned on the railing, needing a few minutes to compose himself, away from her and the pull she so effortlessly exerted on his senses.

He knew she'd be leaving, Massimo reminded himself. This was not something new, or unexpected.

So why did it hurt so much to hear her speak of it in such a cool manner?

The weekend with her had left him raw. Needy.

It had opened his eyes to parts of his own character he wasn't sure he'd even known existed, and cracked open the shell he'd so carefully built around his heart.

Even when he'd kept reminding himself that none of this would last, that she'd soon be gone, that it was supposed to be only sex, Kendra was undermining the very foundations of his life.

Of whom he thought he was, and what he'd always thought he'd wanted.

He didn't want to let her go, even though he fully knew he had no say in the matter.

There was also the frightening thought that it would be easy, should she crook her little finger, to leave what he'd built and follow her wherever she wanted to go.

Of course, it would be anything but easy, and not even possible.

Not just was Minori his home, but he had a responsibility to Nonna, and to Pietro, that tied him to that home even more securely than his deep and abiding love for the Amalfi Coast.

There would be no running off into the sunset. No casting all to the wind in the name of love, even if Kendra had been even the slightest bit interested in him doing so.

Which she was making very clear she was not.

This too was not news, although for the last three days he'd willfully pushed that knowing aside, pretending that somehow, someway, there was a chance for them.

Or, more precisely, a chance that she would fall for him, the way he'd fallen for her, and choose a life together over one of excitement and adventure.

He suppressed a harsh snort at that thought.

For a few moments he'd believed her when she told him he was neither staid nor boring. He'd wanted to believe it. Needed to, as a sop to his ego, and a reason to step out of his comfort zone and give her all she wanted, sexually. Now, looking back on the weekend just ending, he hardly recognized the man he'd been, or pretended to be, when with her. That man had been far bolder and more demanding than Massimo of old had ever been. It had been an illusion—created more for himself, he thought, than for Kendra's benefit. A fantasy of the man he'd always wanted to be.

No, that man had lived a brief existence, and it was time to admit there was no use for him in real life.

Yet, as the ferry drew closer to the dock and Massimo made his way back to his bewitching companion, he had to admit the weekend had fundamentally changed him in other ways.

He'd told himself, over and over, that Therese had been the one. That love at first sight dictated it was so, because hadn't he fallen for her immediately? Now he realized Nonna had been right. He'd been infatuated by a beautiful face and willowy figure and, having placed her on the pedestal of first love, only love, when she'd tumbled off that lofty perch, he'd been convinced his heart was shattered.

Convinced it was impossible to love again.

How terribly, horribly wrong he'd been.

Drawing near to where he'd left Kendra, he saw her in profile, noted the tightness of her lips, the way her fingers grasped the rail, as though to anchor herself, and he paused.

She'd all but told him outright that she was through with him as a lover. When he'd suggested they continue the affair, she'd balked, and he hadn't wanted to listen.

Hadn't wanted to read between the lines and hear what she was saying.

If for no other reason than the love he had for her, he needed to accept that decision. He never wanted to make her uncomfortable, and he certainly didn't want her pity. For eventually she'd realize his feelings, and that would, if nothing else, make things awkward.

Best now to lock away those feelings and try, as best he could, to go back to being the colleague she'd once slept with, and now held at arm's length.

Taking a deep breath, retreating behind the wall she'd all but destroyed, he moved forward, just as the ferry eased into the dock.

He was tempted to touch her arm, but knew that was an impulse born of the very need he had to suppress, so instead he cleared his throat to get her attention.

"I think you're right," he said, as she glanced around at him. "It's best we leave this weekend behind, and go back to the way things were before."

She nodded slowly. "If things were different, we could keep seeing each other, but they're not. So, yes, let's not complicate things any more than we already have."

"Concordato," he agreed, although the word felt like acid in his mouth. "No more complications."

It looked as though she might say something more but instead just nodded again, and turned away to look out at the dock, leaving him to wonder how long it took a shattered heart to mend. If it ever did.

CHAPTER SEVENTEEN

KENDRA HAD ONCE heard someone say that when you're young the days are short, and the years long, but when you're old the days are long and the years short. But it was only now, as her time on the Amalfi Coast was coming to a close, that she truly understood the sentiment. Although, of course, for her it wasn't years that flew by, but weeks.

The days were torturously long, spent as they were almost constantly in Massimo's presence. Even when she couldn't see or hear him, as long as she knew he was around her system stayed on high alert.

It was worse at the villa, even though she'd gone back to her old plan of being there as little as possible. At night, knowing he was just steps away stole whatever scrap of peace she may have otherwise achieved.

Having promised Pietro she would, she still had her breakfast in the kitchen, but nothing would convince her to come in early enough in the evenings to eat dinner with the family. Mornings were hard enough.

Having to put on a smiling face so none of them would realize she was slowly dying inside.

Being treated with cool courtesy by the man who'd once made her feel like the most beautiful woman on earth, who'd made her scream with pleasure and beg for more, was too painful.

Thankfully, she was a master at concealing her agony behind smiles and laughter, although the effort it took to produce either was exhausting.

Whenever anyone at the clinic or in the village asked where she was going when she left Minori, she told them back to Canada, although she hadn't told anyone there that she was coming. The truth was, she didn't know what she was going to do, or where she was going to go, and had no interest in making firm plans.

"You still haven't said where you'll be going next," Koko said, three weeks before Kendra's contract with the clinic would be up. "Usually by now you'd have some kind of plan."

Glad that her cousin couldn't see her face, Kendra chuckled.

"I have some feelers out, and am still doing some research. Besides, I didn't get to see much of the rest of Italy before starting the job, so I'll probably do that before I move on."

Her cousin had accepted her explanation, but

Kendra knew the real reason why she hadn't made plans. There was a tiny, stupid part of her heart still whispering that she should consider staying here, on the Amalfi Coast. That perhaps if she did, somewhere down the road she and Massimo could find a way to work things out.

Definitely a stupid idea.

It wasn't Massimo who was the problem, but her. Even if he wanted her—which didn't seem to be the case—she didn't trust herself to be able to give him what he deserved.

Someone who would stay by his side, and never leave.

A woman he'd want to spend the rest of his life with, instead of one who always seemed to eventually disappoint those she loved, and became disposable.

As that thought flowed through her head, Kendra realized her greatest fear had been realized.

She was in love with Massimo. Deeply, honestly. Truly.

What else could this sensation be? This need to make sure he was happy—that whatever she did was in his best interests, rather than her own. The constant conflict of wanting to be near him, yet having to keep away, so that what happened between them wouldn't end up being a source of pain for him.

Thankfully the revelation came while she lay,

sleepless, in her bed, staring out the window at the moon, which seemed almost close enough to touch. The bright orb wavered, filtered through the tears filling her eyes, but Kendra refused to let them fall. Instead, she blinked them away and clenched her fingers into fists.

This was the life she'd chosen. One that made sense in the context of whom and what she was.

There was no use pretending she could be anything else—anyone else—and that was all there was to it. Wasn't she used to heartbreak? To having to walk away? No matter how she ached at the thought of leaving Massimo—leaving this idyllic life he and his little family lived—doing so was for the best.

For all of them.

Although the flow of tourists had abated, the clinic was still busy, mostly with locals, and Kendra was glad of the workload, even though it often meant working alongside Massimo. Pretending everything was fine and dandy, when just being near him gave her pain a keener edge since she'd admitted to herself the depths of her feelings.

"You're still here, young lady?" Mrs. De Luca asked, as Kendra met her in reception to take her back to the examination room. "I thought you were only in Minori for the summer."

"I leave in a few weeks, but the other, full-time

nurses are taking their holidays now, so I'm filling in until they get back."

"Well, I was talking to some of my friends and we all agree you're the best of the summer nurses we've had over the last few years. Even Amelia Lionetti sings your praises, after you took the time to explain to her about how to manage that sleep disorder she has."

Thankfully, Massimo had been able to determine that Mrs. Lionetti had non-24-hour sleep-wake disorder, rather than Alzheimer's or one of the other possible diagnoses. Getting the elderly lady to understand what that was, and what they would be able to do to help, hadn't been easy, but Kendra had patiently explained until it sunk in.

Hearing she now had the approval of the village *nonne* was gratifying, to be sure, but it did nothing to heal the broken place inside. The void created by love, and the fear it created.

Just as she got Mrs. De Luca into the examination room, Kendra heard the sound of breaking glass coming from reception, raised voices and then a truncated scream.

"Stay here," she told the elderly lady, before running back down the corridor.

The scene that met her eyes had her freezing for a moment, and her perception slowed, so that it felt as though it took minutes, rather than seconds, to survey the room.

One panel of the front door broken.

A woman curled on her side on the floor, unmoving and bleeding, in the shards.

The reception staff and waiting patients frozen in place.

A man she didn't recognize, holding what looked like a metal pipe in one hand and a knife in the other, standing beside the fallen woman.

"I told you not to come here," he said. "I told you to keep quiet." It seemed as though he was talking to the woman on the floor next to him, but his eyes kept darting from side to side, keeping tabs on everyone in the room. "Get up. Get up, damn you."

Strange how the mind works, Kendra thought, still in slow-motion mode, because it was only then she realized the man was speaking in English.

When the woman on the floor didn't move, he shouted again, "Get up!"

He was escalating, the situation becoming more dangerous by the second.

Holding up her hands, Kendra stepped forward.

"Sir," she said, keeping her voice level and firm. "Sir, I need you to calm down. Let me—"

"Shut up! Step back!"

"It's okay," she said, not stopping, but pacing

slowly closer. "It's all right. I'm just going to help you get your friend up, so you can leave."

"No!" That flat gaze, wavering back and forth, then settling on Kendra again. "She's fine. We don't need your help."

Then he glanced down at the woman, and Kendra took what might be her only opportunity.

A side kick catching him just above the diaphragm, hopefully sending it into spasm, was meant to put him down, but didn't. Instead, he staggered backward, hitting the unbroken side of the door, bouncing off and straight at her, teeth bared, knife held high.

He didn't expect her to go low, but that's what she did. Grabbing his leg, using upward momentum to flip him up and over, hearing the clatter as the pipe and the man hit the floor. Spinning around, heart pounding, getting into a fighting stance, watching as he got up again, still holding the knife. Knowing he was about to charge her again. Ready for it.

There was a movement, just a flash in her peripheral vision, and she somehow knew who it was, and what he was going to do. Watched in horror as Massimo rushed forward, flinging one strong arm around the drug-crazed man's neck, putting him in a choke hold.

The knife flashed at least once before Kendra could get to them, and she didn't even care that she'd probably broken the man's wrist when she disarmed him.

But it took the combined strength of both her and Dr. Mancini to get Massimo to let go of the now-unconscious man.

Then it was all a blur. Shouts and motion, a sick sensation when she saw the blood on Massimo's shirt.

"Are you hurt?" she asked him, trying to find the source, checking chest and rib cage, stomach, then grabbing his arm, seeing the gash in his sleeve. In the flesh exposed beneath.

Cursing, holding back the tears, wanting to scream at him, stanching the blood with her hand, since she had nothing else available.

And through it all Massimo didn't move. Didn't say a word. But his chest was heaving, and when she looked up to tell him to come with her so she could examine the gash, he was staring down at her, and the look in his eyes sent a chill down her spine.

Unmistakable fury.

She knew what it was, because she felt the same way.

"You can scream at me later," she said, keeping her teeth clamped together so as not to let loose at him. "But right now, I want you in exam room two so I can examine your wound."

His eyes narrowed, and a muscle ticked in his jaw, then he gave one stiff nod.

"I'm taking Dr. Bianchi to dress his wound," Kendra said to the room at large, not caring if anyone heard or not.

All she cared about was making sure Massimo was all right.

Massimo couldn't speak. Didn't dare say one word, as Kendra unbuttoned his cuff and turned back his sleeve.

He didn't even feel any pain from the slice on his arm. He was still caught in the nightmare of seeing Kendra fighting with a knife-wielding madman. Still filled with the type of rage he hadn't even known himself to be capable of.

She'd told him he could scream at her later, and he hoped she was ready for that, because, oh, yes, it was coming.

In the meantime, it was all he could do to maintain some semblance of sanity.

It had been hard enough over the past weeks to do so, when all he was wrestling with was loving a woman who would soon disappear from his life. This incident—near tragedy—threatened to push him over the mental equivalent of one of the famous cliffs along the Amalfi Coast.

"I knew what I was doing, Massimo." He heard the steel in her voice. Turned his head away, unable to even look at her just then. "I had it under control."

Luckily for her, the door opened just then, and Fredo Mancini came in.

"The police are here, and they'll need to take your statements," he said, coming over to take a look at the wound on Massimo's arm, palpating around it. "Clean slice. Not too deep. Have it cleaned up and some stitches and you'll be fine."

"Can you ask one of the other nurses to take care of it, please, Dr. Mancini?"

Now he couldn't help whipping his head around to look at her, took in her stoic expression, the lines bracketing her mouth and wrinkling the skin between her brows.

"I'll do it myself," Fredo said.

And then Kendra was gone.

"Her hands were shaking." Fredo had his back turned, getting the supplies he needed. "And I'm not surprised." He shook his head, as he pulled on a pair of gloves. "Mine would be too, if I'd just fought a madman like that. I didn't see it, but I heard she was magnificent."

But thankfully, when Massimo made no reply, Fredo lapsed into silence.

They had to close the clinic, of course. Alessio Pisano, who'd been out at the time of the incident, came rushing back to oversee the cleanup and boarding over of the broken door, and sent everyone home.

By the time he'd gotten his stitches, Kendra had already left, taken off by the police to give her statement.

The shock was wearing off, but not the rage. He knew he needed to contain it, but it kept bubbling up, needing release.

Knowing how the village grapevine worked, he made sure to call his grandmother to let her know he was all right, only to find that Kendra had done that for him.

"Oh, Massimo. What a terrible thing. Kendra said you'd been hurt but the wound wasn't serious, and I'm glad she did. I've had so many calls, and the story gets worse each time I hear it. Is it true Kendra fought him off? She didn't mention that when she called. Was she hurt?"

Reassuring Nonna took some doing, and he was exhausted by the attempt.

Exhausted but still furious.

He needed to find Kendra.

For some reason now his mind insisted on playing tricks on him, telling him she wasn't all right. That the scene he remembered in his head, as frightening as it was, wasn't the way it actually happened.

That it was worse, and Kendra had been hurt. Perhaps even killed.

He called, but got no answer from her cell phone, so he hung up and sent a text.

Where are you?

Then, when there was no response, another.

I need to know you're okay.

Finally...

I'm fine. Just needed to clear my head.

Where?

Another seemingly interminable wait, and then:

On the beach.

Of course. If he'd been thinking straight, he would have known she'd head for the water. A place that brought her peace, and reminded her of her father.

He hoped she'd found some of that peace there. For him, for the first time in his life, the familiar surroundings of his beloved home brought no comfort at all.

With rapid strides, he traversed the streets

from the clinic down to the shore, stopping on the boardwalk to search the shoreline, eventually spotting her sitting on the sand near the water. Legs crossed in front of her, head tilted back, her face to the afternoon sun, which dipped toward the horizon a little sooner every day, she should have looked relaxed. But he knew her now. Intimately. Had studied her, even when his brain told him to stop looking, and everything about the line of her back, and the set of her shoulders, screamed tension.

Just like that, as though a switch had been thrown inside, his terrible rage drained away. Oh, he was still angry, but the urge to shout, to lose all control, had waned. Enough that he felt confident to toe off his shoes and, holding them in his hand, walk down to sit beside her.

When he looked over at her, he saw the tear tracks on her cheek, and his heart contracted. Reaching out, he touched her damp skin.

"You scared me," she said, before he could find words. "I was afraid you'd die, and…"

She turned her face away, so that all he saw was the curve of her cheek, the long line of her throat. He waited, wanting to hear what she would say, but she didn't finish her sentence.

He leaned closer, wanting to touch her—*needing* it—but holding himself in check, even when he saw another tear trickle down her cheek.

Then it came to him that although they were to part, although he was not, and never would be, enough for her, if he'd learned one thing today it was that tomorrow was not a given. They would go their separate ways, but, at least on his part, it would be in honesty.

"I was afraid for you too, Kendra. Desperately so. I thought *you* would die and I would have missed my chance to tell you that I love you."

She froze, her face still turned away from him, and another tear trailed down her face.

Wanting to comfort her, not knowing how best to, Massimo touched her shoulder.

"I didn't say that to hurt you, Kendra. Nor do I expect you to say it back to me. I just want you to know."

Then, before he could do or say something he'd regret, he got up and walked away.

CHAPTER EIGHTEEN

KENDRA LET MASSIMO GO.

Not because she didn't want to call him back, or tell him she loved him too, but because the fear was unrelenting.

She knew not admitting she felt the same way would hurt him, and that was the last thing she wanted to do. But hurting him by staying silent was a far smaller pain in the long run than making promises she couldn't keep.

For all intents and purposes, she was better off alone. Living a solitary life meant she didn't risk complications or cause damage to anyone else. Since she was eighteen, she'd only ever had to think about herself. What did she know about being a part of a couple? A part of a family?

Nothing.

Not anything of substance, anyway. Not enough to be sure she could make it work. That she wouldn't screw it all up.

Using the heel of her palm, she swiped at her tears, heartsick.

No. It was better for everyone if she stuck with the plan and left. Kept traveling. Fulfilling that childhood dream, born in the library stacks, museums and concert venues of Toronto. That plan she envisioned all those years ago had given life meaning, even if her life probably was—in other people's eyes—a truncated one.

One without ties to bind or choke and, perforce, without the elusive emotion that seemed to cause nothing but pain to anyone who felt it.

Hadn't it caused the end of her father's dream to be a doctor?

Devastated both hers and Grammy's lives, when Dad died?

Looking back on the plethora of broken homes and dashed dreams she'd seen in her lifetime, she shook her head.

All caused because someone, at some point, fell in love.

Which was all well and good, except love rarely seemed to bring true happiness.

The people she would hurt when it turned out love wasn't enough—when they realized *she* wasn't enough—didn't deserve that pain.

No. No, no, no.

She had to leave before Pietro got attached. Before she succumbed to Nonna's mothering. Before Massimo discovered that she wasn't deserving of the emotional investment he would make.

Because she knew, deep down, that a man as steadfast and true as he would give her his all, in every way. And the fear of what that would do to him if she stayed, and tried, and failed, was too much to bear.

Love, in her mind, meant making the best decisions for those you cared about. Hard choices, but the right ones in the end.

A crisp evening breeze blew off the sea, churning high, gray clouds across the darkening sky, and Kendra lifted her damp cheeks into it, inhaling the scent of the ocean. Where in the past her thoughts would turn to her father, now she knew whenever she was by the water, she'd think of Massimo. Think of the love she came so close to having, and had to walk away from.

It was time to move on, before she caused any more harm to the most wonderful man she'd ever met.

"What are you looking for, when you travel?"

It was as though Massimo still sat beside her, asking the question once more, as he had in Positano the first night they'd officially met.

Once upon a time that had been an easy question to answer.

Adventure.

Freedom.

Meaning.

Now, none of those words had any resonance.

None sparked pleasure. There was a hollow ring to them, as though the drum skin of her life, once so taut and melodic, had been punctured.

Perhaps beyond repair.

Sighing, feeling tears stinging behind her eyes again, she glanced at her watch and was surprised to see how late it had become. Only a pink haze still lay on the horizon, the sun having gone down while she was so lost in thought its setting had gone noticed.

Getting to her feet, she picked up her shoes and knapsack from where she'd left them, and started back toward the clinic to get to her scooter. But, on arrival she realized it was gone, most likely stolen.

"Oh, great."

She was too tired to even curse, knowing it was best to save that energy for the hike to the police station.

"Signorina Kendra."

The voice came from the small café across the street, and she turned to see the proprietor walking quickly toward her, waving both hands over his head.

"Good evening," she said, as he reached her. "Did you by any chance see who took my scooter? It was right here."

"Dr. Massimo paid one of the young men to ride it up to the villa, *signorina*, and asked me to watch for when you came back. After what happened today, he thought perhaps you might prefer to be driven, rather than ride. I have called for a taxi for you already."

"Oh…"

"It is the dinner hour, *signorina*, so I must go back. *Buono notte.*"

As he trotted back across the street, the taxi he'd summoned arrived, and Kendra sank into the back seat with a grateful sigh.

How considerate of Massimo to think of her, even in the midst of his own turmoil and upheaval. He'd been angry—*furious*—with her after the incident earlier. She'd seen it in his eyes, and had prepared herself as well as she could to face it. After all, at the time she'd been furious too.

And more frightened than she'd ever been before. Not for herself, but for him. Seeing the blood on his shirt, knowing that knife wounds inflicted when adrenaline was high sometimes didn't even hurt, and the patient could be slowly bleeding out inside, almost took her to her knees.

A world without Massimo in it was unthinkable.

Just imagining it made her stomach twist and had sweat breaking out on her brow, as the flash of the knife slicing down played behind her eyelids like a sick horror movie scene.

Thankfully, the man driving the taxi didn't

seem inclined to speak, and it was a quiet ride to the villa.

If she'd had to talk about what had happened earlier again, she might burst into tears, and she'd already cried more today than she had since the day her grandmother died. Which was the last and one of a very few times she'd cried as an adult.

Somewhere around the age of twelve, she'd already learned crying didn't help. It was when she'd been moved again, going to her uncle, leaving behind the cousins she'd grown to love, the dog one of the neighbors had gifted her, and the aunt who'd taught her to cook. She'd cried and pleaded to be allowed to stay, but her aunt had just shaken her head.

"Nothing can be done about it, Kendra. It's time to go, and no amount of crying can change that."

No amount of crying can change that.

Harsh words to a little girl, but all too true.

The taxi approached the driveway, and Kendra's heart stuttered at the sight of Massimo's car parked a bit haphazardly in its usual spot.

Where else would he be but at home, you idiot?

Opening the door, she tried to pay, but the taxi driver lifted his hand.

"Dr. Bianchi paid me already, *signorina*."

Even that he'd taken care of. Much of her childhood, and all of her adult life, she'd done everything for herself. No wonder that, on a day as fraught as this one had been, an act of kindness—of care—made her once more well up.

She got out and watched the taxi drive away, taking a few minutes to compose herself before heading toward the house. When she opened the door, there was a screech from the kitchen that froze her blood, and then the sound of a chair falling over. Dropping her bag and starting down the hallway at a run, she saw Pietro round the corner from the kitchen, going as fast as his feet could carry him toward her, his arms outstretched.

Without hesitation, she scooped him up, her heart jackhammering, as she wondered what she'd see in the kitchen...

"Zia Kendra, you're all right!" Pietro was crying into her neck, clinging to her so hard it hurt. "Zio said you were, but I was worried anyway."

"He wouldn't go up to have his bath until he'd seen you for himself." Mrs. Bianchi stood in the doorway to the kitchen, and the anxiety on her face was unmistakable. "We heard what happened, and were both concerned about you."

Wrapping him tighter in her arms, Kendra rocked back and forth, rubbing Pietro's back, in tears again herself. "I'm fine, my sweet boy. I'm fine. Don't cry."

"Let me take him." Mrs. Bianchi came forward, but Kendra shook her head.

"No. No, I've got him. We're all right, aren't we, sweetheart?"

Mrs. Bianchi reached out and touched Kendra's cheek gently, and then nodded toward the kitchen.

"Come through and sit, then. He might not be huge, but Pietro is getting quite big, aren't you, darling?"

The little boy's sobs had abated somewhat, but he was shivering, and Kendra went to the chair in the corner of the kitchen and grabbed the blanket draped over the back. Then she sat down and wrapped it around the thin, trembling shoulders.

Even thus occupied, she looked around, but there was no sign of Massimo.

She wanted to ask where he was, but hesitated. Then she took a deep breath, knowing she had to face him sometime.

"Massimo?"

"He's in the garden. He said he needed some air."

"He looked sad," Pietro whispered into Kendra's neck. "I think his arm was hurting. Will you look after him, Zia?"

Such a simple question. Childlike and innocent.

But for Kendra there were so many layers to it, she didn't know how to answer.

Then something snapped inside her heart, broke apart to release a wave of such sweet pain she bit her lip so as not to make a sound.

It was then, with Pietro's slight weight in her lap, his arms still holding her so tight, and Mrs. Bianchi's worried, motherly gaze on her face, that everything fell into place.

And it all suddenly made sense.

So, she gave Pietro another gentle squeeze, and replied, "I will, Pietro. I will."

It was almost completely dark in the garden, the clouds overhead blocking the moon, the breeze fresh on his face.

Rain was coming. He could smell it on the wind, feel the moisture in the air. It was one of the things his *nonno* had taught him as a little boy. How to read the signs so as to be prepared for whatever came, whether on the land or sea.

Nonno understood weather patterns, and how all of nature interconnected perfectly.

"Except man," Nonno had said with a shake of his head. "Man thinks himself above it all, when we're little better than organized dust and water."

From Nonna he'd learned more about people— how empathy differed from sympathy, and why both were important in life. When to hold his ground, and when to let go.

They'd both emphasized honesty, integrity and

taking care of those around him. They'd guided him through the harsh maze his younger life had been, giving him guidance, acceptance and the love he'd lacked at home. Massimo credited them both with his life path and whatever happiness he'd been able to grasp.

Now, as he sat in the garden one of his ancestors had planted, he wished Nonno was here. Just to talk to. To give him some of that down-to-earth advice.

Massimo shifted, letting his gaze lift to the sky, accepting the pain. Settling into it, knowing it would be with him for a long time.

Probably forever.

He didn't know what he'd expected, when he'd admitted his feelings to Kendra. It wasn't as though he'd thought he had a chance. Yet, although he'd steeled himself for rejection—whether hard or gentle—somehow her silence had hurt even more.

For her, usually so forthright and sure, to not respond at all had been more heartbreaking than he could ever have expected.

A shaft of light flashed for an instance on the grass, then was gone, but he didn't turn around. Nonna, he thought, coming to check on him, to try to coax him inside. Although she wasn't born into a farming family, like her husband, she'd learned the signs and would know it would soon rain. She'd be angry if he stayed out in the damp.

"You once asked me what I was looking for, when I traveled."

His heart leaped, but he didn't turn at the sound of Kendra's voice. He was still too raw, and he didn't want her to know. His response came automatically, as though from someplace deep he had little control over.

"You said adventure, freedom and a wider worldview than the one you grew up with."

"You remember."

She sounded surprised, and that made a harsh chuckle break from his throat. He remembered everything. Too much.

"Yes."

"Well, I want you to forget I said it." She sounded closer, and he was sure he hadn't imagined a soft brush against his shoulder. "I realized today that was bull."

He shook his head, not understanding where the conversation was going. If she was now ready to let him down, he wished she would get it over with.

"Don't you want to hear the real answer?"

He shrugged. "Certainly. If you want to tell me."

"I've been looking for a home. For somewhere

to belong. For someone to love me—just the way I am—and take all the love I have to give."

Soft arms around his neck, her familiar, beloved scent filling his head. A kiss on the top of his head, followed by her twirling a lock of his hair around her finger.

He didn't dare move, or speak.

Or hope.

Yet his heart was pounding, and he had to clench his fingers into fists to stop himself from reaching for her hands.

"I think, if you really love me—not just because we're crazy good together in bed, but all of me—the way I love you, I could find those things here."

That caveat, her lack of surety about his feelings, finally galvanized him. Reaching behind to swing her around, he pulled her into his lap and kissed her until he was sure the moon had fallen from the sky just to shine on them.

When he finally broke the kiss, it was so he could trail his lips to her ear, and say, "The first moment I saw you, at Spiaggia Tordigliano, I fell for you, but refused to admit it. And every time since then I have fallen a little more, until now I can't imagine life without you."

"Massimo." She made his name sound like a song. One only she knew how to sing in the perfect key. "I fought my feelings as hard as I could, afraid, because I'm not sure I know how to be what you want. What you need. I've never been in love before. Didn't really believe in it, until I met you. Suppose I get it wrong, or mess it up?"

He cupped her face, and kissed her gently, wishing now that it weren't so very dark, so he could see her eyes.

"You are perfect in every way, Kendra, and I love you for all you are. Your adventurous spirit, your independence, your laughter and tears. I love you even when you shout at me, or try to punch me because I have given you a fright."

Then he knew he had to admit his own fears. Give her a chance to change her mind.

"But it is I who know I might not be what you need. I can't promise to run off with you to exotic places, should you desire to do so, for my life is here and I am committed to helping so many people."

She laid a finger against his lips.

"My vagabond days are over. All I want is to build a life here with you, if you will have me."

"If I will have you?" He squeezed her against his heart, and heard her sigh. "Now that you have pledged yourself to me, my home will be with you, always."

"Always," she repeated, wrapping her arms around his neck and whispering in his ear, "I like the sound of that."

EPILOGUE

SUMMER HAD COME again to the Amalfi Coast, and the wildflowers in the upper woods were a riot of color, their perfume filling the air.

"Make sure you pick many pink ones for Nonna." Now twelve, Pietro had appointed himself the arbiter of taste, style and comfort at Agriturismo Villa Giovanna. "They are her favorite."

Massimo and Kendra exchanged a look, and when Massimo whispered to her, "You would never believe I've known her more than three times longer than him," Kendra had to laugh.

As the sound echoed into the woods, Massimo's eyes grew hooded, and Kendra shivered, knowing exactly what was on his mind.

Even after four years, he still had the ability to turn her on with a look, and remind her that when it came to love, her laughter was, for him, a constant aphrodisiac.

Moving to where they'd left the wagon they would use to transport the flowers back to the house, Kendra surveyed the bounty destined to grace the villas for their guests to enjoy. Pinks and purples and blues still predominated, with the hot-weather flowers making a slow start this year, because the area had stayed unseasonably cool after Easter.

As they were placing the last of the blooms into the cart, a voice called, "Oo-ee," from the road, and Pietro immediately looked at Massimo.

"That is Tonio," he said. "I told him I would be here this morning."

"Oh?" Massimo raised his brows, and Pietro squirmed slightly.

"Yes. Yesterday he showed me a stream on his father's land and invited me to come and fish in it." His brow creased in that cute, old-mannish way he had. "Although I don't think there is anything to catch. It is a very *small* stream."

"Did you tell Nonna you would be going?"

"I did, and she told me to ask your permission, but I forgot. May I go, anyway?"

Kendra was inclined to say yes, but then she was usually inclined to say yes to Pietro, who was still as sweet, as kind, as he'd ever been. Instead, though, she let Massimo take the lead.

Massimo, the wretch, let the little boy squirm a little, before saying, "I will allow it, but next time you ask in advance, before your friends arrive to whisk you away."

"Yes, Papa." He sounded contrite but couldn't stop himself from doing a little jig. "I will."

"Off you go then."

"Thank you, Papa. Thank you, Mama."

And then, running to hug and kiss them both, he took off at a gallop, his long thin legs flying along, so that he disappeared into the trees in the trice.

"Ah," Massimo said. "That is what summer is about, isn't it?" Wrapping his arms around her waist, he pulled Kendra close, and bent to nip at the base of her throat. "Running wild with friends, fishing in fishless streams, getting filthy."

"Nonna won't be pleased when he tracks mud into her kitchen later," she replied, dancing her fingers down his spine, and smiling when he shuddered.

"Mrs. Bianchi, if you do such things, I will be forced to take my revenge, here and now."

She laughed, looking around, tempted. Then common sense took over.

"Not with a small battalion of preteens running amok around here, our son among them."

It still gave her a thrill to say "our son" that way. They'd had to wait until they were married for three years before they could legally adopt Pietro, but the wait had given them all time to create a new normal.

Pietro had sobbed when she and Massimo had

asked if he was willing for them to adopt him formally, and Kendra had cried right along with him when he vehemently said yes. Massimo had been equally moved, and the sight of the tears he couldn't contain had made Kendra feel as though her heart would burst with love.

Nonna had suggested she move into one of the villas, to let the newlyweds and Pietro have the farmhouse to themselves, but none of them would entertain that idea. With a marked lack of reluctance, Nonna had stayed right where she was, and life settled into a beautiful rhythm.

Kendra was the on-call locum nurse for the clinic, working the summer months and stepping in if any of the other nurses went on holidays or took sick leave. For the rest of the year, she kept busy helping around the villa and farm, learning new recipes and cooking techniques from Nonna, and being Pietro's Mama.

And Massimo's wife—a role she'd found, despite her initial fears, suited her down to the ground.

They were still discussing when and how to expand their family, but neither of them felt the need to rush. Making sure Pietro felt secure had been their main concern. Now that he was, they were talking about trying for a baby, but also considering adopting again.

Kendra had never been happier, and she told Massimo so every chance she got.

"So, if I can't have my way with you against one of these wonderfully handy trees, may I do so later, at a time and a place of your convenience?"

Kendra laughed, and saw his eyes grow even darker, the sight giving her anticipatory goose bumps. He really did know how to turn her on, and keep her simmering.

"I would be very upset if you didn't," she replied demurely. "Very upset indeed."

"Let us go home, then," he said, reaching for the cart's handle.

Overcome with sweet emotion, she touched his arm, and when he turned his midnight gaze her way, she said, "When I'm with you, I am already home."

And immediately found herself exactly where she was happiest. In his arms, held tight against his heart.

"As it is for me," he whispered into her ear, causing a shiver of delight to trickle along her spine. "And will be forever."

* * * * *